The Poems of Emily Dickinson

艾米莉·狄金森诗选
601~900首

[美] 艾米莉·狄金森 著　　周建新 译

·广州·

图书在版编目（CIP）数据

艾米莉·狄金森诗选：601～900首：英汉对照/（美）艾米莉·狄金森（Emily Dickinson）著；周建新译．—广州：华南理工大学出版社，2021.1
ISBN 978-7-5623-6511-2

Ⅰ.①艾… Ⅱ.①艾… ②周… Ⅲ.①诗集-美国-近代-英、汉 Ⅳ.①I712.24

中国版本图书馆CIP数据核字（2020）第247631号

艾米莉·狄金森诗选（601～900首）

（美）艾米莉·狄金森（Emily Dickinson）著　周建新　译

出 版 人：	卢家明
出版发行：	华南理工大学出版社
	（广州五山华南理工大学17号楼，邮编510640）
	http：//www.scutpress.com.cn　E-mail：scutc13@scut.edu.cn
	营销部电话：020-87113487　87111048（传真）
策划编辑：	吴翠微
责任编辑：	陈　蓉
责任校对：	曾映玲
印 刷 者：	广州市新怡印务股份有限公司
开　　本：	787mm×1092mm　1/20　印张：17　字数：368千
版　　次：	2021年1月第1版　2021年1月第1次印刷
定　　价：	49.00元

版权所有　盗版必究　印装差错　负责调换

译者前言

本书一如前两个选译本，是从约翰逊编辑的 1955 年集注版《艾米莉·狄金森诗歌全集》中按顺序选取第 601 至 900 首诗，译为中文，仍取英汉对照体例。约翰逊编的 1955 年集注版与其编的 1960 年阅读版在文本上有些许不同，包括字词、标点等。本书内 300 首诗与 1960 年的阅读版在字词方面的不同，已在附录的对照表中列出，读者可自行查阅。

本书对一些难读、难懂之处提供了题解或注释，但远未涵盖全部。相比于前 600 首，601～900 首大致有两个突出特点：一是形式上较为传统，格律、押韵、分行等形式上的断裂、跳跃较少，因而诗歌相对易读，虽然不一定易懂。601～900 首中一些诗似是缘于现实某个场景或事件的激发，若读者对当时语境不甚了了，则恐难领会作者意图，只能凭想象了，这时作品就几乎完全离开作者，进入读者的阅读视域。二是诗歌情感较少剧烈动荡，较少极喜或狂悲的极端情感宣泄，多现深情、徐缓或冷静（冷峻）叙述之状。其中冷静（冷峻）叙述的诗，似是作者对自身具体经历或感受的总结、反思，更多抽象，不易读懂。写于 1862—1864 年间的 601～900 首诗，显示了作者诗艺的圆熟以及如常人般丰富的情感。

本书译文之不足在所难免，请读者诸君不吝批评指正。

由于艾米莉·狄金森的诗歌一般都没有标题，本书目录中取每首诗第一行做标题，书中诗歌的序号均按约翰逊版中的序号。题解或注释中所引《圣经》原文均来自 King James 版。提及艾米莉·狄金森书信全集中的某一封信时，以"L"开头，后接信的序号。以上提到的约翰逊两个全集本以及狄金森书信全集是指：

Dickinson, Emily. *The Poems of Emily Dickinson：Including Variant Readings Critically Compared with All Known Manuscripts*. Ed. Thomas H.

Johnson. 3 vols. Cambridge, MA: Belknap Press of Harvard University Press, 1955.

Dickinson, Emily. *The Letters of Emily Dickinson*. Eds. Thomas H. Johnson, Theodora Van Wagenen Ward. 3 vols. Cambridge, MA: Belknap Press of Harvard University Press, 1958.

Dickinson, Emily. *The Complete Poems of Emily Dickinson*. Ed. Thomas H. Johnson. Boston: Little, Brown and Company, 1960.

译 者

2020 年 8 月

目 录

601	A still—Volcano—Life—	1
	一座沉寂的——火山——是生命——	1
602	Of Brussels—it was not—	2
	布鲁塞尔地毯——当然不是——	2
603	He found my Being—set it up—	3
	他发现了我的真身——把它竖起——	3
604	Unto my Books—so good to turn—	4
	回到我的书本——多好——	4
605	The Spider holds a Silver Ball	5
	蜘蛛捧一个银球	5
606	The Trees like Tassels—hit—and swung—	6
	树木似流苏——碰撞——摇摆——	7
607	Of nearness to her sundered Things	8
	接近已离去的事物	9
608	Afraid! Of whom am I afraid?	10
	害怕！我害怕谁？	10
609	I Years had been from Home	11
	我已离家多年	12
610	You'll find—it when you try to die—	13
	当你想要死去——你会发现——	14
611	I see thee better—in the Dark—	14
	在黑暗里——我看你看得更清——	15
612	It would have starved a Gnat—	16
	连蚊蚋也会挨饿——	16
613	They shut me up in Prose—	17
	他们把我关进散文——	18
614	In falling Timbers buried—	18
	埋在倾倒的木料深处——	19

615	Our journey had advanced—	20
	我们的旅途向前延伸——	20
616	I rose—because He sank—	21
	我升起——因为他沉落——	21
617	Don't put up my Thread and Needle—	22
	别把我的针线收起——	23
618	At leisure is the Soul	24
	灵魂在闲暇时	25
619	Glee—The great storm is over—	25
	真高兴——狂暴的风雨已结束——	26
620	It makes no difference abroad—	26
	外面并无差异——	27
621	I asked no other thing—	27
	我不再要求其他东西——	28
622	To know just how He suffered—would be dear—	28
	了解他如何受苦——令人宽慰——	29
623	It was too late for Man—	30
	对于人类已经太迟——	31
624	Forever—it composed of Nows—	31
	永远——由无数当前组成——	31
625	'Twas a long Parting—but the time	32
	分离已多年——但会面	33
626	Only God—detect the Sorrow—	33
	唯有上帝——体察悲戚——	34
627	The Tint I cannot take—is best—	34
	我得不到的色彩——最美——	35
628	They called me to the Window, for	36
	他们喊我到窗前,因为	36
629	I watched the Moon around the House	37
	我望着屋旁的月亮	39
630	The Lightning playeth—all the while—	40
	闪电一直——玩乐——	40
631	Ourselves were wed one summer—dear—	41

	我们联姻在一个夏季里——亲爱的—— ……	42
632	The Brain—is wider than the Sky— ……	42
	头脑——比天空辽阔—— ……	43
633	When Bells stop ringing—Church—begins— ……	43
	钟声止息——教堂——才开启—— ……	43
634	You'll know Her—by Her Foot— ……	44
	你会认识她——根据她的脚—— ……	45
635	I think the longest Hour of all ……	46
	我认为世上最漫长的时辰 ……	47
636	The Way I read a Letter's—this— ……	47
	我读信的方法——是这样—— ……	48
637	The Child's faith is new— ……	49
	孩子的信仰清晰—— ……	50
638	To my small Hearth His fire came— ……	50
	他的热火来到我小小的炉膛—— ……	51
639	My Portion is Defeat—today— ……	51
	我的那一份是失败——今天—— ……	52
640	I cannot live with You— ……	53
	我无法与你一起生活—— ……	55
641	Size circumscribes—it has no room ……	57
	宏大自有其限制——它没有空间 ……	57
642	Me from Myself—to banish— ……	58
	把我从自己身上——驱离—— ……	58
643	I could suffice for Him, I knew— ……	59
	我可以满足他，我知道—— ……	59
644	You left me—Sire—two Legacies— ……	60
	主人——你留给我——两份遗产—— ……	60
645	Bereavement in their death to feel ……	61
	对他们去世深感悲痛 ……	61
646	I think to Live—may be a Bliss ……	62
	我觉得活着——可能是一种快乐 ……	63
647	A little Road—not made of Man— ……	64
	一条小路——不是人踩出—— ……	64

648	Promise This—When You be Dying—	65
	请答应这一点——当你奄奄一息——	66
649	Her Sweet turn to leave the Homestead	67
	她甜美的转身要离开宅邸	69
650	Pain—has an Element of Blank—	70
	痛苦——有一种空白的性质——	70
651	So much Summer	71
	如此丰盈的夏季	71
652	A Prison gets to be a friend—	72
	牢笼成了一位朋友——	73
653	Of Being is a Bird	74
	那存在是一只鸟	75
654	A long—long Sleep—A famous—Sleep—	75
	一个长长的——睡眠——一个闻名的——睡眠——	76
655	Without this—there is nought—	76
	没有了这——一切皆空——	77
656	The name—of it—is "Autumn"—	77
	它的名字——叫——"秋天"——	78
657	I dwell in Possibility—	78
	我居住在可能里——	79
658	Whole Gulfs—of Red, and Fleets—of Red—	79
	一湾湾——红,一队队——红——	79
659	That first Day, when you praised Me, Sweet,	80
	那头一天,当你赞美我,亲爱的,	80
660	'Tis good—the looking back on Grief—	80
	这挺好——回顾悲伤——	81
661	Could I but ride indefinite	81
	我愿能无拘无束地游弋	82
662	Embarrassment of one another	83
	互感难堪	83
663	Again—his voice is at the door—	84
	再一次——他的声音在门口响起——	85
664	Of all the Souls that stand create—	86

	从神创造的所有灵魂里——	86
665	Dropped into the Ether Acre—	87
	坠入茫茫苍天——	87
666	Ah, Teneriffe!	87
	啊，特纳利夫！	88
667	Bloom upon the Mountain—stated—	88
	盛开在山巅——壮丽辉煌——	89
668	"Nature" is what we see—	90
	"自然"是我们所见——	90
669	No Romance sold unto	91
	市场上售卖的浪漫故事	91
670	One need not be a Chamber—to be Haunted—	91
	要碰上闹鬼——一个人不必非得是一个房间——	92
671	She dwelleth in the Ground—	93
	她寓居在地里——	93
672	The Future—never spoke—	94
	未来——从不言语——	94
673	The Love a Life can show Below	95
	下界的生活能展示的爱	95
674	The Soul that hath a Guest	96
	有访客的灵魂	96
675	Essential Oils—are wrung—	97
	精油——被榨出——	97
676	Least Bee that brew—	97
	再小的蜜蜂也会酿蜜——	98
677	To be alive—is Power—	98
	活着——就是力量——	98
678	Wolfe demanded during dying	99
	沃尔夫临终前问	99
679	Conscious am I in my Chamber,	100
	我意识到在我房间，	101
680	Each Life Converges to some Centre—	102
	每个生命都向某个中心汇集——	102

681	Soil of Flint, if steady tilled— 坚硬的土地，若经常耕犁——	103 103
682	'Twould ease—a Butterfly— 它能使一只蝴蝶——悠然	104 104
683	The Soul unto itself 灵魂对于它自己	105 105
684	Best Gains—must have the Losses' Test— 最好的收获——必经过失落的考验——	106 106
685	Not "Revelation"—'tis—that waits, 不是"启示"——在——等待，	106 107
686	They say that "Time assuages"— 他们说"时间会冲淡"——	107 107
687	I'll send the feather from my Hat! 我会寄出我帽上的羽毛！	108 108
688	"Speech"—is a prank of Parliament— "演说"——是国会里的恶作剧——	108 109
689	The Zeroes—taught us—Phosphorous— 寒冷到零——让我们了解了——磷——	109 109
690	Victory comes late— 胜利姗姗来迟——	110 110
691	Would you like summer? Taste of ours. 你会喜欢夏季吗？尝尝我们的。	111 111
692	The Sun kept setting—setting—still 太阳不断下降——下降——静悄悄	112 112
693	Shells from the Coast mistaking— 在海边误拿了一些贝壳——	113 113
694	The Heaven vests for Each 上苍赐予每个事物	113 114
695	As if the Sea should part 仿佛大海要分开	115 115
696	Their Height in Heaven comforts not— 他们在高高的天堂也未心安——	116 116
697	I could bring You Jewels—had I a mind to—	117

	我可以带珠宝给你——如果我有意——	117
698	Life—is what we make it—	118
	生活——由我们创造——	119
699	The Judge is like the Owl—	120
	法官就像枭——	120
700	You've seen Balloons set—Have'nt You?	121
	你见过放飞的气球——不是吗?	121
701	A Thought went up my mind today—	122
	今天我脑里涌起一个想法——	123
702	A first Mute Coming—	123
	初次悄悄地到来——	123
703	Out of sight? What of that?	124
	在视线以远?那算啥?	124
704	No matter—now—Sweet—	125
	现在——无关紧要——亲爱的——	125
705	Suspense—is Hostiler than Death—	126
	悬念——比死亡更有敌意——	126
706	Life, and Death, and Giants—	127
	生命,死亡,巨人——	127
707	The Grace—Myself—might not obtain—	127
	上天的恩典——我自己——恐难得到——	127
708	I sometimes drop it, for a Quick—	128
	我有时放下它,为了生存——	128
709	Publication—is the Auction	129
	发表——是一种拍卖	129
710	The Sunrise runs for Both—	130
	日出为那两位而出现——	131
711	Strong Draughts of Their Refreshing Minds	131
	他们新奇思想的醇香	132
712	Because I could not stop for Death—	132
	因为我不能停步等候死神——	133
713	Fame of Myself, to justify,	134
	如果我有声名,是凭真本领,	134

714	Rest at Night	134
	在夜里歇息	135
715	The World—feels Dusty	135
	世界——感觉尘土仆仆	135
716	The Day undressed—Herself—	136
	白日给自己——卸妆——	137
717	The Beggar Lad—dies early—	137
	那乞讨的男孩——死得早——	138
718	I meant to find Her when I came—	139
	我来是为找到她——	139
719	A South Wind—has a pathos	140
	一阵南风——夹着	140
720	No Prisoner be—	140
	不会有牢囚幽闭——	141
721	Behind Me—dips Eternity—	141
	身后——浸染着永恒——	141
722	Sweet Mountains—Ye tell Me no lie—	142
	美丽的群山——你们从不对我说谎——	142
723	It tossed—and tossed—	143
	它颠簸——颠簸——	143
724	It's easy to invent a Life—	144
	发明一个生命很容易——	144
725	Where Thou art—that—is Home—	145
	你在哪里——哪里——就是家——	145
726	We thirst at first—'tis Nature's Act—	146
	最初我们口渴——是自然的行为——	146
727	Precious to Me—She still shall be—	146
	对我很珍贵——她依然是——	147
728	Let Us play Yesterday—	148
	让我们重演昨日——	149
729	Alter! When the Hills do—	150
	改变！当群山可以——	151
730	Defrauded I a Butterfly—	151

	我欺骗了一只蝴蝶——	151
731	"I want"—it pleaded—All its life—	152
	"我想要"——它恳求——要它的终生——	152
732	She rose to His Requirement—dropt	152
	她应和他的要求——抛弃	153
733	The Spirit is the Conscious Ear.	153
	精神是有意识的耳朵。	154
734	If He were living—dare I ask—	154
	他是否还活着——我胆敢问——	155
735	Upon Concluded Lives	156
	对于已完结的生命	156
736	Have any like Myself	156
	有谁像我这样	157
737	The Moon was but a Chin of Gold	158
	月亮仅是金黄下巴一面	159
738	You said that I "was Great"—one Day—	160
	你说我"大"——有一天——	161
739	I many times thought Peace had come	161
	很多次我幻想和平已来到	162
740	You taught me Waiting with Myself—	162
	你教我独自等候——	163
741	Drama's Vitallest Expression is the Common Day	163
	戏剧最生动的体现是那平常日子	164
742	Four Trees—upon a solitary Acre—	165
	四棵树——屹立于一块荒地——	165
743	The Birds reported from the South—	166
	鸟儿们从南方——	167
744	Remorse—is Memory—awake—	168
	懊悔——是记忆——苏醒——	169
745	Renunciation—is a piercing Virtue—	169
	弃绝——是一种令人揪心的德行——	170
746	Never for Society	170
	他对友伴的找寻	171

747	It dropped so low—in my Regard—	172
	它坠得如此低——在我看来——	172
748	Autumn—overlooked my Knitting—	172
	秋天——俯看我织衣——	173
749	All but Death, can be Adjusted—	173
	除了死亡,一切皆可调整——	173
750	Growth of Man—like Growth of Nature—	174
	人的生长——像大自然的生长——	174
751	My Worthiness is all my Doubt—	175
	我的价值在于我全部的质疑——	176
752	So the Eyes accost—and sunder	176
	所以眼神相遇——就分离	177
753	My Soul—accused me—And I quailed—	177
	我的灵魂——声讨我——我感到害怕——	177
754	My Life had stood—a Loaded Gun—	178
	我的生命立着——像一杆上膛的枪——	178
755	No Bobolink—reverse His Singing	179
	没有哪一只食米鸟——停止歌唱	180
756	One Blessing had I than the rest	180
	相比于其余我获得的一个祝福	181
757	The Mountains—grow unnoticed—	182
	群山——不知不觉地长高——	182
758	These—saw Visions—	182
	这些——曾经看到的景象——	183
759	He fought like those Who've nought to lose—	184
	他打起仗来好似他已无可失去——	184
760	Most she touched me by her muteness—	185
	她主要用她的静默将我触动——	186
761	From Blank to Blank—	186
	从荒芜到荒芜——	187
762	The Whole of it came not at once—	187
	整个过程不是一下子完成——	188
763	He told a homely tale	188

	他讲述一个平常的故事	189
764	Presentiment—is that long Shadow—on the Lawn—	189
	预感——是那长长的暗影——在草地上——	190
765	You constituted Time—	190
	你构思时间——	190
766	My Faith is larger than the Hills—	191
	我的信仰大过群山——	191
767	To offer brave assistance	192
	去鼎力相助	192
768	When I hoped, I recollect	192
	我忆起，当我怀着希望	193
769	One and One—are One—	194
	一加一——等于一——	195
770	I lived on Dread—	195
	我靠恐慌而活——	195
771	None can experience stint	196
	没人能领会节省	196
772	The hallowing of Pain	196
	痛苦的神圣	197
773	Deprived of other Banquet, ...	197
	没法参加别人的宴席，	198
774	It is a lonesome Glee—	198
	这是一份孤寂的欢欣——	198
775	If Blame be my side—forfeit Me—	199
	如果是我的错——请将我放弃——	199
776	Purple—	199
	紫——	199
777	The Loneliness One dare not sound—	200
	人不敢探测孤独——	201
778	This that would greet—an hour ago—	201
	这还会打招呼的一位——在一个小时前——	202
779	The Service without Hope—	202
	毫无希望的劳作——	202

780	The Truth—is stirless—	203
	真理——静止——	203
781	To wait an Hour—is long—	204
	等待一小时——太长——	204
782	There is an arid Pleasure—	204
	有一种枯燥的愉悦——	204
783	The Birds begun at Four o'clock—	205
	众鸟在四点开始——	206
784	Bereaved of all, I went abroad—	207
	丧失一切之后，我出走国外——	207
785	They have a little Odor—that to me	208
	他们发出些微的香气——在我心里	208
786	Severer Service of myself	208
	我自己更严苛的工作	209
787	Such is the Force of Happiness—	210
	这就是快乐的威力——	211
788	Joy to have merited the Pain—	211
	很高兴领受了痛苦——	212
789	On a Columnar Self—	213
	倚靠圆柱般的自己——	213
790	Nature—the Gentlest Mother is,	214
	大自然——是最温柔的母亲，	215
791	God gave a Loaf to every Bird—	216
	上帝给每只鸟一块面包——	216
792	Through the strait pass of suffering—	217
	穿过苦难的狭窄通道——	218
793	Grief is a Mouse—	218
	悲伤是一只老鼠——	219
794	A Drop Fell on the Apple Tree—	220
	一滴落在苹果树上——	220
795	Her final Summer was it—	221
	这是她最后一个夏季——	222
796	Who Giants know, with lesser Men	222

	所谓巨人，人类罕见	223
797	By my Window have I for Scenery	223
	在我窗边的风景	224
798	She staked her Feathers—Gained an Arc—	225
	她用她的羽毛做赌注——赢得了一个弧——	226
799	Despair's advantage is achieved	226
	绝望的好处可以获得	227
800	Two—were immortal twice—	227
	二——是两次不朽——	228
801	I play at Riches—to appease	228
	我戏谑财富——以平息	229
802	Time feels so vast that were it not	230
	时间给人感觉如此宽广	230
803	Who Court obtain within Himself	231
	在内心获得朝廷的人	231
804	No Notice gave She, but a Change—	231
	她没给通知，只有一个变化——	232
805	This Bauble was preferred of Bees—	233
	这小玩意深为蜜蜂所喜——	233
806	A Plated Life—diversified	234
	镀过的生命——各异	234
807	Expectation—is Contentment—	234
	期待——是幸福——	235
808	So set it's Sun in Thee	235
	只要它的太阳落在你心里	235
809	Unable are the Loved to die	235
	被爱者不会死去	236
810	Her Grace is all she has—	236
	上天的恩典是她全部所有——	236
811	The Veins of other Flowers	236
	其他花的脉茎	237
812	A Light exists in Spring	237
	一种光明存在于春天	238

813	This quiet Dust was Gentleman and Ladies	239
	这宁静的尘是先生和女士	239
814	One Day is there of the Series	239
	一系列日子中有一个	240
815	The Luxury to apprehend	241
	若说领略什么算奢侈	241
816	A Death blow is a Life blow to Some	242
	对有些人而言死的打击就是生的打击	242
817	Given in Marriage unto Thee	243
	在婚姻里向你臣服	243
818	I could not drink it, Sweet,	243
	我不能喝它，亲爱的，	243
819	All I may, if small,	244
	我所愿，假如很微小，	244
820	All Circumstances are the Frame	244
	所有的环境构成一个框	245
821	Away from Home are some and I—	245
	我和一些人离开家——	245
822	This Consciousness that is aware	246
	感受到邻居和太阳	246
823	Not that We did, shall be the test	247
	并非靠我们已为，作为验证	247
824	The Wind begun to knead the Grass—	247
	风开始揉捏草——	249
825	An Hour is a Sea	250
	一小时是大海一片	250
826	Love reckons by itself—alone—	251
	爱只能——拿自己把自己衡量——	251
827	The Only News I know	251
	我唯一知道的消息	252
828	The Robin is the One	252
	就是那只知更鸟	253
829	Ample make this Bed—	253

	把这张床做得宽敞——	254
830	To this World she returned.	254
	她重回这个世界。	255
831	Dying! To be afraid of thee	255
	即将死去！要害怕你	256
832	Soto! Explore thyself!	256
	索托！探索你自己！	256
833	Perhaps you think me stooping	257
	也许你认为我在弯腰求全	257
834	Before He comes we weigh the Time!	257
	他来之前我们称量时间！	257
835	Nature and God—I neither knew	258
	大自然和上帝——我都不认识	258
836	Truth—is as old as God—	259
	真理——古老如上帝——	259
837	How well I knew Her not	259
	我对她很不熟悉	260
838	Impossibility, like Wine	260
	不可能，就像酒	260
839	Always Mine!	261
	永远属于我！	261
840	I cannot buy it—'tis not sold—	261
	我无法买到它——它不供出售——	262
841	A Moth the hue of this	262
	这种颜色的飞蛾	263
842	Good to hide, and hear 'em hunt!	263
	藏起来真好，听他们来找！	263
843	I made slow Riches but my Gain	264
	我慢慢积攒财富但我的收入	264
844	Spring is the Period	264
	春季是一段时期	265
845	Be Mine the Doom—	265
	毁灭为我所有——	265

846	Twice had Summer her fair Verdure	265
	已经两次夏季给原野	266
847	Finite—to fail, but infinite to Venture—	266
	失败——有限,但冒险无限——	266
848	Just as He spoke it from his Hands	266
	正如他所言出自他的手	267
849	The good Will of a Flower	267
	一朵花的美好心愿	267
850	I sing to use the Waiting	267
	我用等待的时间歌唱	268
851	When the Astronomer stops seeking	268
	当那位天文学家不再探寻	269
852	Apology for Her	269
	为她辩护	269
853	When One has given up One's life	269
	当一个人将生命放弃	270
854	Banish Air from Air—	270
	将空气从空气里驱赶——	271
855	To own the Art within the Soul	271
	在灵魂里拥有	271
856	There is a finished feeling	272
	有一种解脱的感觉	272
857	Uncertain lease—develops lustre	272
	不明确的租约——给时间	273
858	This Chasm, Sweet, upon my life	273
	爱人,我生命中,这个裂口	274
859	A doubt if it be Us	275
	假如我们疑虑	275
860	Absence disembodies—so does Death	275
	缺席制造无形——死亡亦如是	276
861	Split the Lark—and you'll find the Music—	276
	剖开云雀——你会发现音乐——	276
862	Light is sufficient to itself—	277

	光已自我满足——	277
863	That Distance was between Us	278
	我们之间的距离	278
864	The Robin for the Crumb	278
	知更鸟不为那些碎食	278
865	He outstripped Time with but a Bout,	278
	他轻而易举超过时间，	279
866	Fame is the tint that Scholars leave	279
	名声是那色彩	279
867	Escaping backward to perceive	280
	向后逃会看见	280
868	They ask but our Delight—	280
	它们只要求我们快乐——	281
869	Because the Bee may blameless hum	281
	因为蜜蜂可以不受指责随意嗡嗡	282
870	Finding is the first Act	282
	第一幕是找到	283
871	The Sun and Moon must make their haste—	283
	太阳和月亮一定要赶快——	284
872	As the Starved Maelstrom laps the Navies	284
	像饥饿的大漩涡将舰队吞下肚	285
873	Ribbons of the Year—	286
	流年的飘带——	286
874	They won't frown always—some sweet Day	286
	他们不会总是皱眉——某个甜美的日子	287
875	I stepped from Plank to Plank	287
	我从一块木板迈向一块木板	288
876	It was a Grave, yet bore no Stone	288
	这是一座坟墓，但没一块石头	288
877	Each Scar I'll keep for Him	289
	每个疤痕我会为他留存	289
878	The Sun is gay or stark	290
	太阳愉悦还是绷脸	290

879	Each Second is the last 290
	每一刻都是最后一刻 291
880	The Bird must sing to earn the Crumb 291
	鸟儿必须歌唱以挣得面包粒 291
881	I've none to tell me to but Thee 292
	我找不到谁能告诉我除了你 292
882	A Shade upon the mind there passes 293
	一片阴影从心头经过 293
883	The Poets light but Lamps— 293
	诗人们只点亮灯盏—— 294
884	An Everywhere of Silver 294
	某处遍地银光熠熠 294
885	Our little Kinsmen—after Rain 294
	我们细小的亲戚——在雨后 295
886	These tested Our Horizon— 296
	这一些检验我们的地平线—— 296
887	We outgrow love, like other things 296
	我们不再需要爱，像别的东西 297
888	When I have seen the Sun emerge 297
	当我看见太阳出现 297
889	Crisis is a Hair 297
	危机是一根丝发 298
890	From Us She wandered now a Year, ... 299
	离开我们她漂泊至今已一年， 299
891	To my quick ear the Leaves—conferred— 300
	树叶向我敏锐的耳朵——私语—— 300
892	Who occupies this House? 300
	是谁住在这栋房? 302
893	Drab Habitation of Whom? 303
	这是谁淡褐色的住处? 303
894	Of Consciousness, her awful Mate 303
	对于知觉，她可怕的伴侣 304
895	A Cloud withdrew from the Sky 304

	一朵云彩从天空退去 ·································	305
896	Of Silken Speech and Specious Shoe ·········	305
	说柔滑的语言穿俗丽的鞋子 ···························	305
897	How fortunate the Grave— ···················	306
	坟墓多么幸运—— ·································	306
898	How happy I was if I could forget ············	306
	我若能忘记那该多高兴 ·······························	307
899	Herein a Blossom lies— ······················	307
	这里有一枝花—— ·································	307
900	What did They do since I saw Them? ·········	307
	自我见过他们以来他们都干啥? ·····················	308

附录:1955 年集注版与 1960 年阅读版词汇变化一览表 ············ 309

601

A still—Volcano—Life—
That flickered in the night—
When it was dark enough to do
Without erasing sight—

A quiet—Earthquake Style—
Too subtle to suspect
By natures this side Naples—
The North cannot detect

The Solemn—Torrid—Symbol—
The lips that never lie—
Whose hissing Corals part—and shut—
And Cities—ooze away—

601

一座沉寂的——火山——是生命——
闪烁在暗夜——
只要夜够黑
就不会抹去这一切——

隐隐地——大地的震颤——
太轻微而难以察觉
在那不勒斯这边的世界——
北面不可能了解

那庄严——火热的——标记——
那从不撒谎的唇——
它嘶嘶响的珊瑚打开——关闭——
一座座城市——渐次消弭　——

602

Of Brussels—it was not—
Of Kidderminster? Nay—
The Winds did buy it of the Woods—
They—sold it unto me

It was a gentle price—
The poorest—could afford—
It was within the frugal purse
Of Beggar—or of Bird—

Of small and spicy Yards—
In hue—a mellow Dun—
Of Sunshine—and of Sere—Composed—
But, principally—of Sun—

The Wind—unrolled it fast—
And spread it on the Ground—
Upholsterer of the Pines—is He—
Upholsterer—of the Pond—

602

布鲁塞尔地毯——当然不是——
基德明斯特①地毯？否——
风在丛林里买到它——
把它——卖给我

价格适宜——
最穷的——也买得起——
一向节省的乞丐——或小鸟——

---

① 基德明斯特（Kidderminster）：英格兰伍斯特郡（Worcerstershire）一城镇，自 1735 年起便以其生产的双面提花地毯而闻名于世。

也有这个能力

小而馥郁的庭院——
色彩——暗褐而芬芳——
铺满——阳光——和枯叶——
但,主要是——太阳——

风——将它迅速展开——
铺陈在大地——
松林的美化——是他——
也是池塘的——装饰师——

603
He found my Being—set it up—
Adjusted it to place—
Then carved his name—upon it—
And bade it to the East

Be faithful—in his absence—
And he would come again—
With Equipage of Amber—
That time—to take it Home—

603
他发现了我的真身——把它竖起——
扶正——
在上面——刻他的名字——
嘱咐它去往东方

要守信用——当他不在——
他会再来——
马车载满琥珀——
那时——会带它回家——

604

Unto my Books—so good to turn—
Far ends of tired Days—
It half endears the Abstinence—
And Pain—is missed—in Praise—

As Flavors—cheer Retarded Guests
With Banquettings to be—
So Spices—stimulate the time
Till my small Library—

It may be Wilderness—without—
Far feet of failing Men—
But Holiday—excludes the night—
And it is Bells—within—

I thank these Kinsmen of the Shelf—
Their Countenances Kid
Enamor—in Prospective—
And satisfy—obtained—

604

回到我的书本——多好——
在漫长疲惫的白日末尾——
它让斋戒几乎显得亲切——
痛苦——消失于——赞美——

正如香味——振奋久候的宾客
喻示宴会即将开场——
馨香——也催促时间
直至我的小书房——

否则——可能是一片荒野——

不堪的旅人步履杳远——
但假期——驱逐了黑夜——
还有钟鸣——其间——

我感激架上这些亲人——
它们孩童般的脸
让人迷恋——在憧憬时——
满足——由此实现——

605

The Spider holds a Silver Ball
In unperceived Hands—
And dancing softly to Himself
His Yarn of Pearl—unwinds—

He plies from Nought to Nought—
In unsubstantial Trade—
Supplants our Tapestries with His—
In half the period—

An Hour to rear supreme
His Continents of Light—
Then dangle from the Housewife's Broom—
His Boundaries—forgot—

605

蜘蛛捧一个银球
用无形的手——
然后独自曼舞
他的蛛丝展开——悠悠——

他往来于空无——
忙着虚幻的业务——

把我们的挂毯换成它的——
只费一半的工夫——

一小时高超织就
他光的陆地——
就在主妇的扫帚上荡悠——
忘记了——他的疆域——

606
The Trees like Tassels—hit—and swung—
There seemed to rise a Tune
From Miniature Creatures
Accompanying the Sun—

Far Psalteries of Summer—
Enamoring the Ear
They never yet did satisfy—
Remotest—when most fair

The Sun shone whole at intervals—
Then Half—then utter hid—
As if Himself were optional
And had Estates of Cloud

Sufficient to enfold Him
Eternally from view—
Except it were a whim of His
To let the Orchards grow—

A Bird sat careless on the fence—
One gossipped in the Lane
On silver matters charmed a Snake
Just winding round a Stone—

Bright Flowers slit a Calyx
And soared upon a Stem
Like Hindered Flags—Sweet hoisted—
With Spices—in the Hem—

'Twas more—I cannot mention—
How mean—to those that see—
Vandyke's Delineation
Of Nature's—Summer Day!

606①

树木似流苏——碰撞——摇摆——
恍惚一支幽歌
起自微小的众生
与太阳应和——

夏日遥远的琴音——
令耳朵着迷
但总不能让人完全满意——
虽然最杳远的——往往最美丽

太阳有时显露无遗——
然后半遮脸——最后完全隐匿——
仿佛他自己也很随意
拥有乌云的领地

足以将他包围
永远不再显现——
除非他有时兴起
想要扩大果园——

---

① 第291首诗表达了类似的看法，即技艺再高超的画家也无法完全展现大自然的美丽。

一只鸟在篱笆上悠然坐着——
有人在小巷里絮叨
那银色的故事迷住了一条蛇
它将一块石头紧紧缠绕——

鲜艳的花朵绽开花萼
蹿上一根枝头
像被压抑的旗——美美地升起——
芳香馥郁——在花瓣四周——

还有更多——我无法一一提及——
多么平淡无奇——对于那些观众——
见识过范·戴克①描绘的
大自然的——夏季!

607

Of nearness to her sundered Things
The Soul has special times—
When Dimness—looks the Oddity—
Distinctness—easy—seems—

The Shapes we buried, dwell about,
Familiar, in the Rooms—
Untarnished by the Sepulchre,
The Mouldering Playmate comes—

In just the Jacket that he wore—

---

① 范·戴克(Sir Anthony Van Dyck, Van Dyck 亦拼写为 Vandyke, 1599—1641),弗兰芒族巴洛克风格画家(Flemish baroque painter),擅长肖像和风景画,是英国国王查理一世时期(1625—1649)的英国宫廷首席画家。查理一世及其皇族的许多著名画像都是他创作的,最著名的是《查理一世行猎图》(Charles I at the Hunt, c. 1635)(藏于卢浮宫博物馆)。他的画像轻松高贵的风格,影响了英国肖像画将近 150 年。他还创作了许多圣经故事和神话题材的作品,并改革了水彩画和蚀刻版画的技法。

Long buttoned in the Mold
Since we—old mornings, Children—played—
Divided—by a world—

The Grave yields back her Robberies—
The Years, our pilfered Things—
Bright Knots of Apparitions
Salute us, with their wings—

As we—it were—that perished—
Themself—had just remained 'till we rejoin them—
And 'twas they, and not ourself
That mourned.

607①
接近已离去的事物
灵魂自有特殊的时间——
当昏暗的天光——看起来怪异——
其清晰——也容易——显现——

我们埋下的那些肉体,就住在附近,
还那样熟悉,在房间里——
未受坟墓的玷污,
那枯朽的玩伴姗然而至——

仍穿着过去的上衣——
它早已被压在墓底
自从我们——在曾经的清晨,孩提时——一起游戏——
就被一个世界——隔离——

坟墓归还她所抢掠——

---

① 第445首也有类似结尾:死者期待生者加入他们。

流年，交出偷窃我们的东西——
魅影中明亮的星点
向我们敬礼，以其羽翼——

仿佛——是我们——亡故——
他们——则驻留直至我们再次加入——
所以是他们，而不是我们
在哀哭。

608

Afraid! Of whom am I afraid?
Not Death—for who is He?
The Porter of my Father's Lodge
As much abasheth me!

Of Life? 'Twere odd I fear [a] thing
That comprehendeth me
In one or two existences—
Just as the case may be—①

Of Resurrection? Is the East
Afraid to trust the Morn
With her fastidious forehead?
As soon impeach my Crown!

608

害怕！我害怕谁？
不是死神——谁知他是谁？
我父亲小屋的看门人
同样使我羞愧！

---

① 本行在1960年阅读版中改为：As Deity decree—（一如神的旨意——）。富兰克林版则选用本行。

害怕生命?真奇怪我会害怕这东西
它将我纳于
一种或两种存在里——
一如情况所示——

害怕复活?难道东方
会害怕给予黎明
它精致的前额?
那我才会质疑我的王冠!

609

I Years had been from Home
And now before the Door
I dared not enter, lest a Face
I never saw before

Stare solid into mine
And ask my Business there—
"My Business but a Life I left
Was such remaining there?"

I leaned upon the Awe—
I lingered with Before—
The Second like an Ocean rolled
And broke against my ear—

I laughed a crumbling Laugh
That I could fear a Door
Who Consternation compassed
And never winced before.

I fitted to the Latch
My Hand, with trembling care
Lest back the awful Door should spring
And leave me in the Floor—

Then moved my Fingers off
As cautiously as Glass
And held my ears, and like a Thief
Fled gasping from the House—

609

我已离家多年
如今站在家门前
不敢迈步,唯恐遇见一张
从未见过的脸

直勾勾瞪着我
问我所来何事——
"我想知道我遗下的一段生活
是否还保留在此?"

我倚靠着畏惧——
徘徊于从前——
那一刻像大海翻卷
撞击在耳边——

我发出战战兢兢的笑声
竟在一扇门前怯弱
曾经直面多少惊心动魄
从未有过退缩。

我轻触门闩
颤抖的手,小心翼翼
唯恐可怕的门反弹
把我关在屋里——

然后移开手指
小心如移动玻璃
随后捂住耳朵,像小偷
从那屋子仓皇逃离——

610

You'll find—it when you try to die—
The Easier to let go—
For recollecting such as went—
You could not spare—you know.

And though their places somewhat filled—
As did their Marble names
With Moss—they never grew so full—
You chose the newer names—

And when this World—sets further back—
As Dying—say it does—
The former love—distincter grows—
And supersedes the fresh—

And Thought of them—so fair invites—
It looks too tawdry Grace
To stay behind—with just the Toys
We bought—to ease their place—

610①

当你想要死去——你会发现——
更容易放手现在——
若忆起那虽已离去——
而你仍不舍的人——你明白。

虽然他们的空位会被填补——
一如他们大理石的名字
被青苔覆盖——但它们绝不可能占满——
你仍可选些新名字——

如果今世——进一步回溯——
如死前所言的——确可重来——
那前世的爱——会变得更精彩——
会将当前的替代——

对他们的思念——如此甜美诱人——
难免显得过谦
若落在后面——与我们买的玩具
待在一起——以免将他们的空位挤占——

611

I see thee better—in the Dark—
I do not need a Light—
The Love of Thee—a Prism be—
Excelling Violet—

---

① 题解：人临死前若想起已死去的亲爱的人，并念念不忘，则会更容易放手今世。去世的爱人在活着的人心里总会留下一个空位，同时活着的人也会再选新的爱人，但新旧爱人都不可能独自占满那个空位。若时光能够倒流，回到从前，回到当时亲爱的人还在世时，那旧爱会显得更鲜明精彩，肯定会把当前的新爱替代。对旧爱的思念如此甜蜜诱人，如果不敢勇敢、大胆去怀想，只敢留在当前（"落在后面"），和新爱［Toy（玩具）］在一起，觉得这样就不会挤占旧爱留下的空位，这当然显得高雅（Grace），但不免高雅过了头（tawdry），显得过谦了。

I see thee better for the Years
That hunch themselves between—
The Miner's Lamp—sufficient be—
To nullify the Mine—

And in the Grave—I see Thee best—
It's little Panels be
Aglow—All ruddy—with the Light
I held so high, for Thee—

What need of Day—
To Those whose Dark—hath so—surpassing Sun—
It deem it be—Continually—
At the Meridian?

611

在黑暗里——我看你看得更清——
我不需要光明——
对你的爱——就是一块棱镜——
胜过紫罗兰的芳馨——

这些年我看你看得更清
它们之间相互彰显——
矿工的矿灯——已足够——
把矿藏照得耀眼——

在坟墓里——我看你看得最清——
它狭小的四壁
红红的——发出——光明
我站得很高，为了看你——

白日还有何必要——
如果对某些人来讲——黑暗——远胜太阳——

它认为自己——一直以来——
就是正午时光?

612

It would have starved a Gnat—
To live so small as I—
And yet I was a living Child—
With Food's necessity

Upon me—like a Claw—
I could no more remove
Than I could coax a Leech away—
Or make a Dragon—move—

Not like the Gnat—had I—
The privilege to fly
And seek a Dinner for myself—
How mightier He—than I—

Nor like Himself—the Art
Upon the Window Pane
To gad my little Being out—
And not begin—again—

612

连蚊蚋也会挨饿——
像我过得如此微小——
可我是个活生生的孩童——
食物必不可少

这对我——犹如一只利爪——
我无法将它扫除

也不能劝服一只水蛭离开——
或请一只巨龙——移步——

我也不像蚊蚋——那样——
有能力飞翔
为自己寻一顿美餐——
他比我——更有力量——

也不像他——有技艺
贴着窗玻璃
挤出卑微的自我——
再不像从前那样——生活——

613

They shut me up in Prose—
As when a little Girl
They put me in the Closet—
Because they liked me "still"—

Still! Could themself have peeped—
And seen my Brain—go round—
They might as wise have lodged a Bird
For Treason—in the Pound—

Himself has but to will
And easy as a Star
Look down upon Captivity—①
And laugh—No more have I—

---

① 本行在1960年阅读版中改为：Abolish his Captivity—

613①

他们把我关进散文——
正如在小女孩的年龄
他们把我放入壁橱——
因为希望我"安静"——

安静!假如他们窥探——
看见我的头脑——四处游弋——
他们该是明智地把一只鸟
关进了牢笼——因为叛逆——

他只会整天向往
如星星般惬意
蔑视对他的束缚——
然后大笑——我不必更努力——

614

In falling Timbers buried—
There breathed a Man—
Outside—the spades—were plying—
The Lungs—within—

Could He—know—they sought Him—
Could They—know—He breathed—
Horrid Sand Partition—
Neither—could be heard—

---

① 题解:不论像小时被关在壁橱还是像如今被关进散文,只不过像一只鸟儿被关入鸟笼,鸟儿一样可用头脑自由思考,用心自由向往,蔑视现实的束缚,如星星一般惬意。如此这般的自由,"我"已觉足够,无需更多努力去争取更多。第657首也提到了"散文"(Prose)。艾米莉·狄金森曾经跟她的侄女玛蒂(Mattie,即Martha Gilbert Dickinson Bianchi, 1866—1943)说过:"Matty, child, no one could ever punish a Dickinson by shutting her up alone."(参见 Bianchi, Martha Dickinson. *Emily Dickinson Face to Face*: *Unpublished Letters with Notes and Reminiscences*. Boston:Houghton Mifflin Company, 1932:65-66.)

Never slacked the Diggers—
But when Spades had done—
Oh, Reward of Anguish,
It was dying—Then—

Many Things—are fruitless—
'Tis a Baffling Earth—
But there is no Gratitude
Like the Grace—of Death—

614①
埋在倾倒的木料深处——
一个男人气息奄奄——
外面——无数铁锹——挥舞——
想挖出一个空间——在里面——

愿他——知道——他们在救他——
愿他们——知道——他气息奄奄——
可怕的沙土将他们隔离——
相互——听不见——

挖土者毫不气馁——
但当铁锹停下——
啊,得到痛心的回馈,
只见死亡——在那——

许多努力——徒劳无益——
这个世界扑朔幻变——
但没有什么感激
能比拟死亡的——恩典——

---

① 题解:一如第 566 首诗中的说话人未能及时给老虎带来水,未能拯救濒临死亡的老虎,本诗中的救人者也未能成功救活被埋的人。但是,他们的失败却也给被埋者带来了死亡的恩典,这是唯一值得感恩的。

615

Our journey had advanced—
Our feet were almost come
To that odd Fork in Being's Road—
Eternity—by Term—

Our pace took sudden awe—
Our feet—reluctant—led—
Before—were Cities—but Between—
The Forest of the Dead—

Retreat—was out of Hope—
Behind—a Sealed Route—
Eternity's White Flag—Before—
And God—at every Gate—

615

我们的旅途向前延伸——
我们的双足即将跟上
抵达存在路上那个偏僻的岔口——
那是永恒——用术语来讲——

我们的脚步突然畏缩——
我们的双足——不愿——前进——
之前——都是闹市——但如今这中间地带——
是死者的森林——

撤退——已无希望——
身后——一条封闭的路——
永恒的白旗——在前方——
上帝——等在每个入口处——

616

I rose—because He sank—
I thought it would be opposite—
But when his power dropped—
My Soul grew straight.

I cheered my fainting Prince—
I sang firm—even—Chants—
I helped his Film—with Hymn—

And when the Dews drew off
That held his Forehead stiff—
I met him—
Balm to Balm—

I told him Best—must pass
Through this low Arch of Flesh—
No Casque so brave
It spurn the Grave—

I told him Worlds I knew
Where Emperors grew—
Who recollected us
If we were true—

And so with Thews of Hymn—
And Sinew from within—
And ways I knew not that I knew—till then—
I lifted Him—

616

我升起——因为他沉落——
我原以为会这样对立——

但当他的力量萎缩——
我的灵魂却僵直无力。

我给虚弱的王子鼓励——
我坚定——平稳地——唱诵——
我用圣歌——帮他驱走薄翳——

当露水散尽
它们曾让他的额头僵硬——
我遇见了他——
互诉贴心话——

我告诉他那最美好——须穿过
这肉体低矮的拱门之路——
没有哪个凡夫如此勇敢
敢于拒绝坟墓——

我告诉他我所了解的世界
那是王者辈出之地——
他们会记起我们
假如我们真心实意——

然后凭着圣歌的魅力——
和我体内的力气——
用我原本不知我已掌握的方法——直到此时——
我才将他抬起——

617

Don't put up my Thread and Needle—
I'll begin to Sew
When the Birds begin to whistle—
Better Stitches—so—

These were bent—my sight got crooked—
When my mind—is plain
I'll do seams—a Queen's endeavor
Would not blush to own—

Hems—too fine for Lady's tracing
To the sightless Knot—
Tucks—of dainty interspersion—
Like a dotted Dot—

Leave my Needle in the furrow—
Where I put it down—
I can make the zigzag stitches
Straight—when I am strong—

Till then—dreaming I am sewing
Fetch the seam I missed—
Closer—so I—at my sleeping—
Still surmise I stitch—

617①
别把我的针线收起——
我将要缝纫
当鸟儿们开始鸣啼——

---

① 关于本诗的写作日期，约翰逊版标为 1862 年，富兰克林版认为是 1863 年。艾米莉·狄金森在 1864 年 6 月初写给文学导师托马斯·希金森（Thomas Wentworth Higginson, 1823—1911）的一封信中说："I was ill in September, and since April, in Boston, for a Physician's care."（L290）事实上，她确曾在 1864 年（8 个月）和 1865 年（6 个月）共 2 次到马萨诸塞州的剑桥（Cambridge, Massachusetts），由波士顿的眼科医生亨利·威廉（Henry W. Williams）治疗眼疾（现在一般认为是虹膜炎）。1864 年的那一次治疗一直持续到 11 月，她住在剑桥东边 4 英里外的波士顿的两位表妹弗朗西丝·诺克罗斯（Frances Norcross, 1847—1919）和路易莎·诺克罗斯（Louisa Norcross, 1842—1896）家里。另参见第 827 首诗的注释。

最好就开始——穿针——

这些很累人——我的眼神要跟着拐来拐去——
当我的大脑——僵直
我就做缝补——这是女王做的活计
不必羞于从事——

围边——太精细
妇女也难以找到那隐形的线结——
卷褶——细细密密——
像斑斑点点的世界——

把针留在线道上——
我就放下休息——
我能把弯曲的针脚
弄直——如果我够力气——

直到那时——仍然幻想在缝纫
在查找哪里漏缝针——
盯得更近——以至——在昏昏欲睡的时辰——
以为自己还在穿针——

618

At leisure is the Soul
That gets a Staggering Blow—
The Width of Life—before it spreads
Without a thing to do—

It begs you give it Work—
But just the placing Pins—
Or humblest Patchwork—Children do—
To Help it's Vacant Hands—

618①

灵魂在闲暇时
会感到巨大打击——
生命的宽广——在展开前
无所事事——

它恳求你给它活计——
但只有穿针引线——
或孩童们做的——最低微的缝衣——
才能解决它双手的空闲——

619

Glee—The great storm is over—
Four—have recovered the Land—
Forty—gone down together—
Into the boiling Sand—

Ring—for the Scant Salvation—
Toll—for the bonnie Souls—
Neighbor—and friend—and Bridegroom—
Spinning upon the Shoals—

How they will tell the Story—
When Winter shake the Door—
Till the Children urge—
But the Forty—
Did they—come back no more?

Then a softness—suffuse the Story—
And a silence—the Teller's eye—
And the Children—no further question—
And only the Sea -reply—

---

① 可与第 443 首诗对照阅读。

619
真高兴——狂暴的风雨已结束——
四个——已回到陆地——
四十个———起沉入——
沉入翻腾的沙里——

摇响铃——为渺茫的救亡——
敲丧钟——为那些美丽的魂灵——
邻居——朋友——还有新郎——
在浅滩上忙转不停——

他们将如何讲述——
当冬天摇晃着门板——
孩子们在催促——
但那四十个——
他们——真的不再回返?

随后的故事——弥漫着温馨——
叙述者的眼睛——布满安宁——
孩子们——不再提问——
只有大海——回应——

620
It makes no difference abroad—
The Seasons—fit—the same—
The Mornings blossom into Noons—
And split their Pods of Flame—

Wild flowers—kindle in the Woods—
The Brooks slam—all the Day—
No Black bird bates his Banjo—
For passing Calvary—

Auto da Fe—and Judgment—
Are nothing to the Bee—
His separation from His Rose—
To Him—sums Misery—

620

外面并无差异——
四季——同样——相宜——
清晨的花朵开到正午——
鲜艳的花苞绽露无遗——

野花——红遍了山林——
溪水欢戏——整日里——
没有一只黑鸟会调低琴音——
当经过耶稣受难地①——

死刑——和最后审判日——
对蜜蜂毫无意义——
与亲爱的玫瑰别离——
已给了它——无尽的悲戚——

621

I asked no other thing—
No other—was denied—
I offered Being—for it—
The Mighty Merchant sneered—

Brazil? He twirled a Button—

---

① 耶稣受难地（Calvary）：即髑髅地，指耶稣被钉上十字架的地方，位于耶路撒冷以西的一座山上。参见《圣经·新约·路加福音》第 23 章第 33 节记载："And when they were come to the place, which is called Calvary, there they crucified him, and the malefactors, one on the right hand, and the other on the left."（Luke 23：33）

Without a glance my way—
"But—Madam—is there nothing else—
That We can show—Today?"

621

我不再要求其他东西——
也没别的什么——被拒绝——
我就为它——投入了自己——
那强大的商人表示不屑——

巴西？他转动一个按钮——
也不往我这边看一眼——
"可是——女士——难道就没别的东西——
我们可以展示给你——今天？"

622

To know just how He suffered—would be dear—
To know if any Human eyes were near
To whom He could entrust His wavering gaze—
Until it settle broad—on Paradise—

To know if He was patient—part content—
Was Dying as He thought—or different—
Was it a pleasant Day to die—
And did the Sunshine face his way—

What was His furthest mind—Of Home—or God—
Or what the Distant say—
At news that He ceased Human Nature
Such a Day—

And Wishes—Had He Any—
Just His Sigh—Accented—

Had been legible—to Me—
And was He Confident until
Ill fluttered out—in Everlasting Well—

And if He spoke—What name was Best—
What last
What One broke off with
At the Drowsiest—

Was He afraid—or tranquil—
Might He know
How Conscious Consciousness—could grow—
Till Love that was—and Love too best to be—
Meet—and the Junction be Eternity

622①
了解他如何受苦——令人宽慰——
了解是否有人类的眼睛在旁边作陪
他可以安放游移的眼光在他们身上——
直到稳稳定格于——天堂——

了解他是否淡定——从容地别离——
是否如他所愿地死去——或有所差异——
死去的那天是否天气晴好——
他一路上是否艳阳高照——

他最后关心的是什么——是家园——或上帝——

---

① 艾米莉·狄金森对死亡的好奇，在其信件中也有表达。1853 年 3 月 24 日，狄金森的好朋友本杰明·牛顿（Benjamin Franklin Newton, 1821—1853）死于肺结核。她在 1854 年 1 月 13 日给本杰明的牧师爱德华·黑尔（Edward Everett Hale, 1822—1909）写信，信中说道："I often have hoped to know if his last hours were cheerful, and if he was willing to die …Please Sir, to tell me if he was willing to die, and if you think him at Home. I should love so much to know certainly, that he was today in Heaven."（L153）

或远方的人怎么看——
当知道他不再是人类
在那一天——

他是否有什么——愿望——
只有他深切的——叹息——
是我——了如指掌——
他是否有信心
直到疾病振翅飞出——在永恒的深井——

假如他开口——哪个名字最好——
哪个在最后
谁跟什么分手
在昏睡最沉的时候——

他是否害怕——或平静——
他是否所知甚详
意识里的意识——如何膨胀——
直到曾经的爱——和难以企及的至爱——
相遇——那邂逅之地就是永生所在

623

It was too late for Man—
But early, yet, for God—
Creation—impotent to help—
But Prayer—remained—Our Side—

How excellent the Heaven—
When Earth—cannot be had—
How hospitable—then—the face
Of our Old Neighbor—God—

623

对于人类已经太迟——
但，对于上帝，还早——
创世——也无助益——
但至少——我们还可——祈祷——

天堂多令人心仪——
当尘世——无法居停——
那时——我们的旧邻——上帝
他的脸——多热情——

624

Forever—it composed of Nows—
'Tis not a different time—
Except for Infiniteness—
And Latitude of Home—

From this—experienced Here—
Remove the Dates—to These—
Let Months dissolve in further Months—
And Years—exhale in Years—

Without Debate—or Pause—
Or Celebrated Days—
No different Our Years would be
From Anno Domini's—

624①
永远——由无数当前组成——

---

① 艾米莉·狄金森很早就开始关注"永远"或"永恒"。她在1846年1月31日写的信中就有提及："Does not Eternity appear dreadful to you. I often get thinking of it and it seems so dark to me that I almost wish there was no Eternity."（L10）1882年11月写的信中也有谈及："I cannot tell how Eternity seems. It wraps around me like a sea [while I do my work]."（L875）她在信件中谈及"eternity"共16次。

它并非不同的时间概念——
只是没有终点——
以及空间无限——

从这一点——可以体会到——
该把日期移入——这些当前——
让月消融在接踵而来的月里——
让年——流失于年——

如果没有辩论——或停顿——
或特别的纪念日——
每年并无不同
自公元元年始——

625

'Twas a long Parting—but the time
For Interview—had Come—
Before the Judgment Seat of God—
The last—and second time

These Fleshless Lovers met—
A Heaven in a Gaze—
A Heaven of Heavens—the Privilege
Of one another's Eyes—

No Lifetime—on Them—
Appareled as the new
Unborn—except They had beheld—
Born infiniter—now—

Was Bridal—e'er like This?
A Paradise—the Host—
And Cherubim—and Seraphim—
The unobtrusive Guest—

625

分离已多年——但会面
时间——已至——
就在最后审判日上帝的宝座前——
这是最后一次——也是第二次

这些无形的爱恋者相见——
凝望一下天堂——
升入这天堂中的天堂——这特权
是他们各自眼中的渴望——

他们没有——生命期限——
着装如初来乍现
尚未真正降生——除了这一次他们看清——
他们被赋予的生命——更加无限——

婚礼——是否也如此?
天国——主持者——
小天使——以及六翼天使——
还有那位谦谦宾客——

626

Only God—detect the Sorrow—
Only God—
The Jehovahs—are no Babblers—
Unto God—

God the Son—Confide it—
Still secure—
God the Spirit's Honor—
Just as sure—

626
唯有上帝——体察悲戚——
唯有上帝——
耶和华们——不会胡言乱语——
对上帝——

是圣子——泄密——
他依然得享——
圣灵的荣誉——
一如既往——

627
The Tint I cannot take—is best—
The Color too remote
That I could show it in Bazaar—
A Guinea at a sight—

The fine—impalpable Array—
That swaggers on the eye
Like Cleopatra's Company—
Repeated—in the sky—

The Moments of Dominion
That happen on the Soul
And leave it with a Discontent
Too exquisite—to tell—

The eager look—on Landscapes—
As if they just repressed
Some Secret—that was pushing
Like Chariots—in the Vest—

The Pleading of the Summer—

That other Prank—of Snow—
That Cushions Mystery with Tulle,
For fear the Squirrels—know.

Their Graspless manners—mock us—
Until the Cheated Eye
Shuts arrogantly—in the Grave—
Another way—to see—

627
我得不到的色彩——最美——
那种颜色难得一遇
我可以摆在集市里——
看一眼——收费一基尼①——

那精细——曼妙的阵势——
在眼前夸显恢宏
像埃及艳后的仆从——
重现——天空——

灵魂顿感
一阵压迫
生出了不满
太微妙——难以诉说——

急切的目光——把田野望遍——
似乎它们在压制
某个秘密——它悄悄向前
像战车——蒙在帆布里——

---

① 基尼（Guinea）：1663 年英国发行的一种金币，1 基尼等于 21 先令，即 1 英镑 1 先令（1.05 英镑），于 1813 年停止流通。

夏季的恳诉——
直指白雪的——其他恶作剧——
它用薄纱把神秘盖住,
害怕松鼠们——知悉。

他们来去无踪的作风——是对我们的嘲弄——
直至被蒙骗的眼
傲慢地闭上——在坟墓里——
这是看的——另一表现——

628

They called me to the Window, for
"'Twas Sunset" —Some one said—
I only saw a Sapphire Farm—
And just a Single Herd—

Of Opal Cattle—feeding far
Upon so vain a Hill—
As even while I looked—dissolved—
Nor Cattle were—nor Soil—

But in their stead—a Sea—displayed—
And Ships—of such a size
As Crew of Mountains—could afford—
And Decks—to seat the skies—

This—too—the Showman rubbed away—
And when I looked again—
Nor Farm—nor Opal Herd—was there—
Nor Mediterranean—

628

他们喊我到窗前,因为

"正是日落时分"——有人说——
我只见一片蔚蓝的农场——
和唯一的一群——

乳白色的牛——吃草
在遥远缥渺的山岗——
以至于当我定睛——它就消失掉——
不再见牛——和土地的模样——

代替它们的——是大海——显现——
还有船只——那么大
群山全做船员——都能容纳——
甲板——天空坐得下——

这些——也——被陈列者抹去——
当我再看第二眼——
不见农场——乳白的牛群——在那里——
也不见地中海波光潋滟

629

I watched the Moon around the House
Until upon a Pane—
She stopped—a Traveller's privilege—for Rest—
And there upon

I gazed—as at a stranger—
The Lady in the Town
Doth think no incivility
To lift her Glass—upon—

But never Stranger justified
The Curiosity
Like Mine—for not a Foot—nor Hand—

Nor Formula—had she—

But like a Head—a Guillotine
Slid carelessly away—
Did independent, Amber—
Sustain her in the sky—

Or like a Stemless Flower—
Upheld in rolling Air
By finer Gravitations—
Than bind Philosopher—

No Hunger—had she—nor an Inn—
Her Toilette—to suffice—
Nor Avocation—nor Concern
For little Mysteries

As harass us—like Life—and Death—
And Afterwards—or Nay—
But seemed engrossed to Absolute—
With shining—and the Sky—

The privilege to scrutinize
Was scarce upon my Eyes
When, with a Silver practise—
She vaulted out of Gaze—

And next—I met her on a Cloud—
Myself too far below
To follow her superior Road—
Or it's advantage—Blue—

629
我望着屋旁的月亮
直至在一块窗玻璃——
她停下——歇息——这是旅人的权利——
就在那里

我凝视——像望一位陌生人——
城里的这位女士
并不觉无礼
举起望远镜——注视——

从没有陌生人
像我这样
好奇——因她无脚——无手——
也无——固定形状——

只像一颗头颅——一个断头台
悄悄滑远——
独自,泛着琥珀黄——
在夜空高悬——

或像一朵无茎之花——
在滚滚大气中坚不可摧
由奥妙的引力支撑——
而非哲学家繁琐的描绘——

她不感——饥饿——也无旅店——
供她——洗漱——
没有嗜好——不关注
谜一般的细碎事物

诸如困扰我们的——生——和死——
以及死后世界——抑或不再有——

似乎只凝思于绝对之物——
伴着清辉——天上遨游——

仔细搜索的特权
不必劳驾我双眼
当她,以一个银色的动作——
就跳出我的视线——

随后——我见她自一片云中突出——
我在下界太远
无法追踪她高空的路途——
或领会美妙的——蔚蓝——

630

The Lightning playeth—all the while—
But when He singeth—then—
Ourselves are conscious He exist—
And we approach Him—stern—

With Insulators—and a Glove—
Whose short—sepulchral Bass
Alarms us—tho' His Yellow feet
May pass—and counterpass—

Upon the Ropes—above our Head—
Continual—with the News—
Nor We so much as check our speech—
Nor stop to cross Ourselves—

630

闪电一直——玩乐——
但当他歌唱——那时——
我们才意识到他存在——

于是我们接近他——凝神屏气——

披绝缘衣——戴手套——
他短促——阴森的低响
令我们惊恐——虽然他黄色的脚
可能走远——又折返——

我们头顶的——绳索——
不断——传来消息——
我们不至于不敢言说——
也不会停下在胸前画十字——

631

Ourselves were wed one summer—dear—
Your Vision—was in June—
And when Your little Lifetime failed,
I wearied—too—of mine—

And overtaken in the Dark—
Where You had put me down—
By Some one carrying a Light—
I—too—received the Sign.

'Tis true—Our Futures different lay—
Your Cottage—faced the sun—
While Oceans—and the North must be—
On every side of mine

'Tis true, Your Garden led the Bloom,
For mine—in Frosts—was sown—
And yet, one Summer, we werc Queens—
But You—were crowned in June—

631

我们联姻在一个夏季里——亲爱的——
你的出现——是在六月——
当你可怜楚楚的生命结束,
我的——也——精疲力竭——

在你曾迷倒我的黑暗里——
我被掳去——
被某位举着一束光的人——
我——同样——得到那块标记。

确实——我们的未来各异——
你的小屋——正对太阳——
而海洋——和北方——
围着我屋房

确实,你的庭园众花芬芳,
而我的——霜冻——遍地——
不过,在一个夏季里,我们都成了女王——
但你——是在六月登基——

632

The Brain—is wider than the Sky—
For—put them side by side—
The one the other will contain
With ease—and You—beside—

The Brain is deeper than the sea—
For—hold them—Blue to Blue—
The one the other will absorb—
As Sponges—Buckets—do—

The Brain is just the weight of God—
For—Heft them—Pound for Pound—
And they will differ—if they do—
As Syllable from Sound—

632

头脑——比天空辽阔——
因为——把他们并排一起——
一个会把另一个包含
轻易地——此外——还有你——

头脑比大海深邃——
因为——让他们——蓝对蓝——
一个会把另一个吸纳——
像海绵——把桶中水——吸干——

头脑和上帝同等重量——
因为——称一称———磅对一磅——
他们的差异——如果有——
就像音节不同于声响——

633

When Bells stop ringing—Church—begins—
The Positive—of Bells—
When Cogs—stop—that's Circumference—
The Ultimate—of Wheels.

633

钟声止息——教堂——才开启——
钟声的——积极意义—

轮齿①——停止——才正式周而复始——
这是轮子的——真义。

634

You'll know Her—by Her Foot—
The smallest Gamboge Hand
With Fingers—where the Toes should be—
Would more affront the Sand—

Than this Quaint Creature's Boot—
Adjusted by a Stem—
Without a Button—I c'd② vouch—
Unto a Velvet Limb—

You'll know Her—by Her Vest—
Tight fitting—Orange—Brown—
Inside a Jacket duller—
She wore when she was born—

Her Cap is small—and snug—
Constructed for the Winds—
She'd pass for Barehead—short way off—
But as She Closer stands—

So finer 'tis than Wool—
You cannot feel the Seam—

---

① 轮齿（Cog）：第 1717 首有 "…the cogs/Of that revolving reason" 的表述。本诗中的 "轮齿"（Cog）乃虚指，即生命或世界轮回之轮中的轮齿，是生命或世界进程中的关键时刻或节点。当生命或世界转动到这个轮齿时停止，生命就从此生轮转入来生，世界由尘世转入天堂。"Circumference" 在狄金森的诗中是多义词，在这里可指周而复始的轮回，即轮齿停止了，轮回就开启了，开启了由此入彼的时刻。这就是生命或世界轮回之轮转动的真正意义，即自来于尘之后，再归于尘，进入彼岸。

② "c'd" 在 1960 年阅读版中改为 "could"。

Nor is it Clasped unto of Band—
Nor held upon—of Brim—

You'll know Her—by Her Voice—
At first—a doubtful Tone—
A sweet endeavor—but as March
To April—hurries on—

She squanders on your Head①
Such Threnodies of Pearl—
You beg the Robin in your Brain
To keep the other—still—

634
你会认识她——根据她的脚——
那橙黄色的纤手
上面的手指——假如换成脚趾——
会让沙粒更难受——

比起这位奇异生灵的靴——
适应一根细茎的大小——
没有靴扣——我断定——
穿进一只毛茸茸的脚——

你会认识她——根据她的上衣——
贴身——橙黄——棕褐——
夹在一件更暗的外套里——
她生来就这般穿着——

她的帽子小巧——舒适——
专为挡风而设计——

---

① "Head" 在 1960 年阅读版中改为 "Ear"。

她会脱帽经过——很快消失——
但当她靠近站立——

它比羊毛还要纤细——
感觉不到缝合线——
既不攒成一簇——
也不起——毛边——

你会认识她——根据她的歌声——
起初——曲调凝重——
一次温柔的努力——但就像三月
过渡到四月——匆匆——

她唱响在你头顶
这支珍珠的挽歌——
你敦请脑中的知更鸟
让大家保持——安静——

635

I think the longest Hour of all
Is when the Cars have come—
And we are waiting for the Coach—
It seems as though the Time

Indignant—that the Joy was come—
Did block the Gilded Hands—
And would not let the Seconds by—
But slowest instant—ends—

The Pendulum begins to count—
Like little Scholars—loud—
The steps grow thicker—in the Hall—
The Heart begins to crowd—

Then I—my timid service done—
Tho' service 'twas, of Love—
Take up my little Violin—
And further North—remove.

635

我认为世上最漫长的时辰
莫过于车厢①已经到站——
而我们正在等候马车——
仿佛时间

感到愤慨——欢乐要来——
竟把金色的指针卡住——
也不让秒针摆——
但最缓慢的一刹——终于结束——

钟摆开始数数——
像一群小学者般——声音洪亮——
脚步声越来越响——在大堂——
心开始膨胀——

我——完成了胆怯的事务——
虽然这些事务，是关于爱恋——
我拿起我的小提琴——
走向——北方以远。

636

The Way I read a Letter's—this—

---

① 车厢（Cars）：原文"Cars"或可指列车的客车厢，则下一行的"Coach"可指到车站接人的四轮马车，如此，则本诗表达的是在家等待访客到来的情形：列车已到站，去车站接人的马车还没载访客回来，这紧张等待的时间最显漫长。最后，等待的时间结束，客人到了厅堂。此时，一直在家为心爱的人到来做准备的期盼者，迫不及待地拿起小提琴出去迎接。

'Tis first—I lock the Door—
And push it with my fingers—next—
For transport it be sure—

And then I go the furthest off
To counteract a knock—
Then draw my little Letter forth
And slowly pick the lock—

Then—glancing narrow, at the Wall—
And narrow at the floor
For firm Conviction of a Mouse
Not exorcised before—

Peruse how infinite I am
To no one that You—know—
And sigh for lack of Heaven—but not
The Heaven God bestow—

636
我读信的方法——是这样——
首先——把门锁住——
再用手指推一下——接着——
以便我能全神贯注——

然后走到最远的角落
以抵消敲门的干扰——
随后把小信件掏出
慢慢把封口撬——

接着——眯眼扫视，墙壁——
再眯眼看看地板
确信没有老鼠
尚未被驱赶——

仔细品读自己有多浩瀚
对于你而非他人——你对此了如指掌——
然后感慨没有天堂——但不是指
上帝恩赐的天堂——

637

The Child's faith is new—
Whole—like His Principle—
Wide—like the Sunrise
On fresh Eyes—
Never had a Doubt—
Laughs—at a Scruple—
Believes all sham
But Paradise—

Credits the World—
Deems His Dominion
Broadest of Sovereignties—
And Caesar—mean—
In the Comparison—
Baseless Emperor—
Ruler of Nought,
Yet swaying all—

Grown bye and bye
To hold mistaken
His pretty estimates
Of Prickly Things
He gains the skill
Sorrowful—as certain—
Men—to anticipate
Instead of Kings—

637

孩子的信仰清晰——
完整——像他的本质——
宽广——像太阳升起
纯净的眼里——
从无疑虑——
嘲笑——犹疑——
笃信所有的欺诳
除了天堂——

对世界充满信心——
以为他管辖
最广阔的王国——
而凯撒——不值一提——
相比之下——
只是无根基的皇帝——
统治虚无，
却控制全部——

一点点成长
从错误地坚持
他天真的估计
对棘手的事项
他学会了技巧
令人难过——毫无疑问——
他将成——人
而不是王——

638

To my small Hearth His fire came—
And all my House aglow

Did fan and rock, with sudden light—
'Twas Sunrise—'twas the Sky—

Impanelled from no Summer brief—
With limit of Decay—
'Twas Noon—without the News of Night—
Nay, Nature, it was Day—

638①
他的热火来到我小小的炉膛——
让蓬荜生辉
要摇扇和打滚,因这突来的光芒——
这就是初升的太阳——这就是天空的景象——

并非从夏日的短暂里升起——
带着消退的期限——
这是正午——毫无黑夜的讯息——
不,大自然,这是白天——

639
My Portion is Defeat—today—
A paler luck than Victory—
Less Paeans—fewer Bells—
The Drums don't follow Me—with tunes—
Defeat—a somewhat slower—means—
More Arduous than Balls—

---

① 题解:Judith Farr 认为本诗是一首情诗,并把诗中"Impanelled"和"brief"两个法律词汇与艾米莉·狄金森作为律师的父亲和哥哥联系起来,认为狄金森这两个用词或许是受了哥哥和父亲的影响(见 Farr, Judith. *The Passion of Emily Dickinson*. Cambridge, Massachussets: Harvard University Press, 1992. 195.)。*Emily Dickinson Lexicon* 解释"impanel"一词有 draped、veiled、covered with curtains、fit as with panels 之意。但在本诗中,恐更接近 enroll 之意,译文取引申义。

Tis populous with Bone and stain—
And Men too straight to stoop again,
And Piles of solid Moan—
And Chips of Blank—in Boyish Eyes—
And scraps of Prayer—
And Death's surprise,
Stamped visible—in Stone—

There's somewhat prouder, over there—
The Trumpets tell it to the Air—
How different Victory
To Him who has it—and the One
Who to have had it, would have been
Contenteder—to die—

639

我的那一份是失败——今天——
比胜利的运气苍白一点——
没这么多赞歌——少一些钟声响起——
没有鼓跟在我身后——敲着——
失败——是一项相对缓慢的——工作——
比舞会①费力——

到处是骨头和污渍——
男人们太刚直难以屈尊第二次②，
堆砌着痛苦的哀伤——
眼珠泛白——在稚嫩的眼里——
祈祷断断续续——

---

① 舞会（Ball）：或指胜利后的庆祝舞会，以与失败相对。原文"Ball"或也可指 pinball，即弹球戏，以与战争相对。

② 既指战士们尸体僵硬，无法弯曲，也指他们有不屈的勇气或气概。

死神的惊奇①,
如清晰的标记——在石头上②——

但有某种更令人自豪的东西,在那里——
小号告诉给空气——
胜利的后果有多迥异
对于赢者——和那
该赢的人,他恐怕
会更欣慰地③——死去——

640

I cannot live with You—
It would be Life—
And Life is over there—
Behind the Shelf

The Sexton keeps the Key to—
Putting up
Our Life—His Porcelain—
Like a Cup—

Discarded of the Housewife—
Quaint—or Broke—
A newer Sevres pleases—
Old Ones crack—

I could not die—with You—
For One must wait

---

① 既指死者脸上惊异的表情僵硬,也可能喻指死神的惊异表情,因为战争导致了这么多伤亡。
② 形容表情清晰而僵硬,如刻在石头上一样。
③ 在胜利中死去,会更感欣慰,可惜是失败而死。在胜利中活着和在胜利中死去,两种胜利有极大差异。

To shut the Other's Gaze down—
You—could not—

And I—Could I stand by
And see You—freeze—
Without my Right of Frost—
Death's privilege?

Nor could I rise—with You—
Because Your Face
Would put out Jesus'—
That New Grace

Glow plain—and foreign
On my homesick Eye—
Except that You than He
Shone closer by—

They'd judge Us—How—
For You—served Heaven—You know,
Or sought to—
I could not—

Because You saturated Sight—
And I had no more Eyes
For sordid excellence
As Paradise

And were You lost, I would be—
Though My Name
Rang loudest
On the Heavenly fame—

And were You—saved—
And I—condemned to be
Where You were not—
That self—were Hell to Me—

So We must meet apart—
You there—I—here—
With just the Door ajar
That Oceans are—and Prayer—
And that White Sustenance—
Despair—

640
我无法与你一起生活——
这就是生活——
而生活就在那边——
架子后面的角落

教堂司事掌管着钥匙——
收起
我们的生活——他的瓷器——
像一个杯子——

被主妇遗弃——
老旧——或破烂——
新的讨人欢喜——
旧的兀自心酸——

我无法与你一起——死去——
因为一个要等着
为另一个合眼——
你——做不到——

而我——能否站在旁边
看着你——冰凉——
自己却没有寒霜的权利——
死去的特权？

我也无法与你一起——复活——
因为你的脸
会把耶稣的脸遮蔽——
那新的恩典

光芒寂寥——又陌生
映照我怀旧的眼——
除非你比他的光辉
更近我身边——

他们会猜测我俩——怎会这样——
因为你——侍奉上苍——你知道，
或设法努力——
而我无法做到——

因为你已充满我视野——
我再没眼力去关切
诸如天国般
卑鄙的卓越

假如你迷茫，我也同样——
虽然在天堂
我的名声
最响亮——

假如你——得救——
而我——被罚去
没有你之地——

那个自己——就是我的地狱——

所以我们只能远远相见——
你在那边——我——在这边——
门半掩
那是海洋——以及祈愿——
还有那白色的滋养——
绝望——

641

Size circumscribes—it has no room
For petty furniture—
The Giant tolerates no Gnat
For Ease of Gianture—

Repudiates it, all the more—
Because intrinsic size
Ignores the possibility
Of Calumnies—or Flies.

641①

宏大自有其限制——它没有空间
容纳琐碎的家具——
巨人不会容忍蚊蚋

---

① 题解：关于原文中的"size"，据 *Emily Dickison Lexicon*，既有"尺寸"（measure）、"空间"（dimension）、"容量"（capacity），也有"周长"（circumference）、"范围"（scope）等意。根据上下文，"size"或指大的尺寸，即"宽广"或"宏大"。如此，诗歌或指"宏大"自有其限制，即既会对自己做出限制也会被自己所限制。一方面，"宏大"不会容留琐碎之物，一如巨人，为了自身感到舒适，不会容忍蚊蠓之类的小昆虫，这是"宏大"对自身的限制；另一方面它也受自身的限制，比如它受天生具有的内在的宏大特性所限，不可能会理睬苍蝇或流言蜚语之类的细碎烦扰。读完本诗，中国读者或许容易联想到一句俗语："大人有大量。"心怀宽广的人，内心不会有琐碎繁杂之累，也不会受外部琐碎繁杂之扰。

为了自身的适意——

别理这一套,不管怎样——
因为内心的宏大已定
不会在乎诽谤
或苍蝇的——可能性。

642

Me from Myself—to banish—
Had I Art—
Impregnable my Fortress
Unto All Heart—

But since Myself—assault Me—
How have I peace
Except by subjugating
Consciousness?

And since We're mutual Monarch
How this be
Except by Abdication—
Me—of Me?

642

把我从自己身上——驱离——
假如我有妙计——
我的要塞就坚不可侵
对于所有的心——

但既然我自己——攻击我——
我怎会有安宁之日
除非压制
意识?

而既然我俩各是君王
这一切怎会成现实
除非退位——
让我离开——我的位子？

643

I could suffice for Him, I knew—
He—could suffice for Me—
Yet Hesitating Fractions—Both
Surveyed Infinity—

"Would I be Whole" He sudden broached—
My syllable rebelled—
'Twas face to face with Nature—forced—
'Twas face to face with God—

Withdrew the Sun—to Other Wests—
Withdrew the furthest Star
Before Decision—stooped to speech—
And then—be audibler

The Answer of the Sea unto
The Motion of the Moon—
Herself adjust Her Tides—unto—
Could I—do else—with Mine?

643

我可以满足他，我知道——
他——也可以满足我——
然而因为担心微小——双方
寻求无限多——

"我能否就是全部"他突然这么说——

我用话语反击——
现在是面对自然——被迫——
现在是面对上帝——

把太阳收藏——到其他西方——
也不让最远那颗星出现
在决定——屈尊发言之前——
这样——更能听见

大海回应
月亮的运行——
调整海潮的——涨落——
我能——对自己——做点什么？

644

You left me—Sire—two Legacies—
A Legacy of Love
A Heavenly Father would suffice
Had He the offer of—

You left me Boundaries of Pain—
Capacious as the Sea—
Between Eternity and Time—
Your Consciousness—and Me—

644

主人——你留给我——两份遗产——
爱是其中之一
天父也会满足
假如他被给予——

你留给我无边的痛苦——
如大海般浩瀚——

在时间与永恒之间——
你的意识——和我之间——

645
Bereavement in their death to feel
Whom We have never seen—
A Vital Kinsmanship import
Our Soul and theirs—between—

For Stranger—Strangers do not mourn—
There be Immortal friends
Whom Death see first—'tis news of this
That paralyze Ourselves—

Who, vital only to Our Thought—
Such Presence bear away
In dying—'tis as if Our Souls
Absconded—suddenly—

645①
对他们去世深感悲痛
虽然我们从未谋面——
有一种紧密的牵连
在我们和他们的灵魂——之间——

陌生人——不会对陌生人哀戚——
有一种不朽的友伴
死神首先接见——正是这个消息

---

① Eberwein 认为本诗可能是对 Elizabeth Barrett Browning（1806—1861）的悼亡诗。（参见 Eberwein, Jane Donahue. *Dickinson: Strategies of Limitation*. Amherst: University of Massachusetts Press, 1985. 221.）约翰逊版指出本诗写于 1862 年，富兰克林版认为是写于 1863 年。

让我们全身瘫痪——

这样的人,仅对我们的思想至关重要——
这样的存在形失影消
在死亡里——就仿佛我们自己的灵魂
突然——潜逃——

646

I think to Live—may be a Bliss
To those who dare to try—
Beyond my limit to conceive—
My lip—to testify—

I think the Heart I former wore
Could widen—till to me
The Other, like the little Bank
Appear—unto the Sea—

I think the Days—could every one
In Ordination stand—
And Majesty—be easier—
Than an inferior kind—

No numb alarm—lest Difference come—
No Goblin—on the Bloom—
No start in Apprehension's Ear,
No Bankruptcy—no Doom—

But Certainties of Sun—
Midsummer—in the Mind—
A steadfast South—upon the Soul—
Her Polar time—behind—

The Vision—pondered long—
So plausible becomes
That I esteem the fiction—real—
The Real—fictitious seems—

How bountiful the Dream—
What Plenty—it would be—
Had all my Life but been Mistake
Just rectified—in Thee

646

我觉得活着——可能是一种快乐
对敢于尝试的人——
这超乎我的想象——
也无法证实——用我的唇——

我觉得我从前携带的心
可以扩大——直至在我看来
那另一颗,像那段小堤岸
面向——大海——

我觉得日子——每个人
都能一天一天忍受——
越高贵——越容易——
相比平凡的一类——①

没有无声的警报——以免产生滋扰——
没有妖魔——在花间游荡——
没有骚动在忧虑的耳边,
没有崩溃——没有死亡——

---

① 这一节的译文也可能是:我觉得日子——可能每一天/ 都是神圣的存在——/ 越高贵——越突显——/ 相比平凡的一类——

但肯定有太阳——
仲夏——在脑间——
不变的南方——在心上——
她的寒冷时光——在后面——

这种景象——我想望已久——
理据貌似足够
以至我误认虚构——为真——
真——仿佛虚构——

多绚丽的梦——
多丰富——看起来——
假如我的一生是个错误
愿在你身上——得到更改

647

A little Road—not made of Man—
Enabled of the Eye—
Accessible to Thill of Bee—
Or Cart of Butterfly—

If Town it have—beyond itself—
'Tis that—I cannot say—
I only know—no Curricle that rumble there
Bear Me—

647

一条小路——不是人踩出——
眼睛看得见它——
可以通往蜜蜂的座驾——
或蝴蝶的车马——

是否有城镇——在前面——

这一点——很难说——
我只知——不会有马车驶向那边
载着我——

648

Promise This—When You be Dying—
Some shall summon Me—
Mine belong Your latest Sighing—
Mine—to Belt Your Eye—

Not with Coins—though they be Minted
From an Emperor's Hand—
Be my lips—the only Buckle
Your low Eyes—demand—

Mine to stay—when all have wandered—
To devise once more
If the Life be too surrendered—
Life of Mine—restore—

Poured like this—My Whole Libation—
Just that You should see
Bliss of Death—Life's Bliss extol thro
Imitating You—

Mine—to guard Your Narrow Precinct—
To seduce the Sun
Longest on Your South, to linger,
Largest Dews of Morn

To demand, in Your low favor
Lest the Jealous Grass
Greener lean—Or fonder cluster

Round some other face—

Mine to supplicate Madonna—
If Madonna be
Could behold so far a Creature—
Christ—omitted—Me—

Just to follow Your dear feature—
Ne'er so far behind—
For My Heaven—
Had I not been
Most enough—denied?

648①
请答应这一点——当你奄奄一息——
会通知我到身边——
让我听到你最后的叹气——
让我——合上你的眼——

不用硬币——虽已铸就
自皇帝手里——
而用我的双唇——唯一的搭扣
是你低垂的双眼——所需——

当一切已四散——我会留驻——
再努力一遍
看那生命是否已完全交出——
我的生命——会回返——

像这般斟上——我全部的奠酒——
这样你就能看到

---

① 与第 622 首诗的主题类似。

死之欢愉——这是生之欢愉在颂赞
通过效仿你——

让我——守卫你狭小的领地——
招引阳光
让大滴的晨露,恒久流连,
在你的南方

这样做,是为了你谦卑的请求
以免嫉妒的小草
萋萋招摇——或紧聚成簇
在其他脸庞四周围绕——

让我向圣母玛利亚求情——
如果玛利亚在
会远远看见一个生灵——
基督——对我——不理睬——

我只要跟随你可爱的身影——
不落后太远——
去往我的天堂——
我难道不是一直
几乎已够多——被拒绝?①

649

Her Sweet turn to leave the Homestead
Came the Darker Way—
Carriages—Be Sure—and Guests—too—
But for Holiday

---

① 这一节表明说话者在对方活着时被对方多次拒绝,未得享人间天堂之福,现在终于可以跟随对方了。

'Twas more pitiful Endeavor
Than did Loaded Sea
O'er the Curls attempt to caper
It had cast away—

Never Bride had such Assembling—
Never kinsmen kneeled
To salute so fair a Forehead—
Garland be indeed—

Fitter Feet—of Her before us—
Than whatever Brow
Art of Snow—or Trick of Lily
Possibly bestow

Of Her Father—Whoso ask Her—
He shall seek as high
As the Palm—that serve the Desert—
To obtain the Sky—

Distance—be Her only Motion—
If 'tis Nay—or Yes—
Acquiescence—or Demurral—
Whosoever guess—

He—must pass the Crystal Angle
That obscure Her face—
He—must have achieved in person
Equal Paradise—

649①

她甜美的转身要离开宅邸
从一条路黑漆漆——
来了车马——毫无疑问——还有客人——确实——
但只是来度假期

这种努力颇为可怜
甚于盈盈海洋
试图起舞翩跹
在它已驱走的海波上——

从未有新娘有这样的典礼——
从未有亲戚下跪
向如此美丽的前额致意——
其实花环的光辉——

更适宜她的脚——在我们眼里——
胜过任一个额前
用雪的技艺——或百合花的巧计
装扮

关于她父亲——不论谁问起——
他只能往高处寻觅
高高如棕榈——在沙地——
好将天空尽收眼底——

远方——是她唯一的动力——
不论它存在——或不存在——

---

① 题解：这是一位姑娘的葬礼，她要离开家园，去往天堂，获得新生，因此也可以视为新娘，但这种情况也颇显可怜，令人同情。这既是葬礼也如婚礼的典礼，有亲戚到来如度假而非悲悼，有人下跪，有人觉得花环应放在死者脚旁而非额上。无论如何，姑娘的目标是远方的天堂，不论你信与不信，若有人想追求她，想问她父亲的意见，那就只能往高处去找寻，要穿过天空，亲自到天堂去问。

默认——或异议——
不论谁怎么猜——

他——一定要穿过水晶角①
它模糊了她的脸庞——
他——一定要亲身抵达
同样的天堂——

650

Pain—has an Element of Blank—
It cannot recollect
When it begun—or if there were
A time when it was not—

It has no Future—but itself—
It's Infinite contain
It's Past—enlightened to perceive
New Periods—of Pain.

650②

痛苦——有一种空白的性质——
它无法记起
它何时开始——或是否有
不痛苦的时期——

它没有未来——只有它自己——
它的无限包含

---

① 水晶角（Crystal Angle）：指天空、天顶，即尘世与天堂（或生与死）接壤之处或边界。据 *Emily Dickinson Lexicon*，"Angle" 可以有这些意思："vertex; intersecting point; limit; border; boundary; edge; [fig.] veil; point between life and death"。

② 题解：痛苦是一种无限期的空白状态，不是阶段性的，换言之，如果只是且总是痛苦，痛苦就是一体的，就不存在过去或未来的说法。它的无限已包含了过去，也足以启发人去想象新的痛苦情形。

它的过去——足以启发人想象
痛苦的——新阶段。

651

So much Summer
Me for showing
Illegitimate—
Would a Smile's minute bestowing
Too exorbitant

To the Lady
With the Guinea
Look—if She should know
Crumb of Mine
A Robin's Larder
Would suffice to stow—

651

如此丰盈的夏季
由我来展现
这不太合理——
是否给一个轻轻的笑靥
已高出预期

对那位女士
身上带着基尼
看——假如她明白
我的那些琐碎
一个知更鸟的食柜
已足够装载——

652

A Prison gets to be a friend—
Between it's Ponderous face
And Ours—a Kinsmanship express—
And in it's narrow Eyes—

We come to look with gratitude
For the appointed Beam
It deal us—stated as our food—
And hungered for—the same—

We learn to know the Planks—
That answer to Our feet—
So miserable a sound—at first—
Nor ever now—so sweet—

As plashing in the Pools—
When Memory was a Boy—
But a Demurer Circuit—
A Geometric Joy—

The Posture of the Key
That interrupt the Day
To Our Endeavor—Not so real
The Cheek of Liberty—

As this Phantasm Steel—
Whose features—Day and Night—
Are present to us—as Our Own—
And as escapeless—quite—

The narrow Round—the Stint—
The slow exchange of Hope—

For something passiver—Content
Too steep for lookinp up—

The Liberty we knew
Avoided—like a Dream—
Too wide for any Night but Heaven—
If That—indeed—redeem—

652①

牢笼成了一位朋友——
在它沉重的脸
和我们的之间——有一种亲缘——
而在它眯长的双眼——

我们心怀感激地找寻
那束约定的光
它光顾我们——犹如我们的食品——
同样——令人渴望——

我们学会熟悉那些木板——
它们应和我们的脚——
声音如此凄惨——起先——
即使现在——也没那么美妙——

---

① 题解：久因于牢笼之人自然熟悉牢笼，所以就成了朋友。狭长的门缝或窗缝上射进来的光，令人如渴望食品般渴望。也熟悉了牢笼的木地板和地板上狱卒来回走动的声音，起先觉得凄惨，久而久之，门外来往巡回的脚步声，就显得更安静些，逐渐给人一些期盼，一点空洞的欢欣和沉醉，不像原先听起来那么凄惨，但无论如何不会像孩提时在池中泼水那样美妙。白天牢门上钥匙插入，貌似是对我们期盼自由的努力的回应，但事实并非如此，所谓自由，其真实度还不如日夜所见的眼前的钢铁牢门，似乎已属于牢中人，也似乎无法避开了。牢门上固定的圆锁、狭长的钥匙孔，每日开锁时圆锁缓慢的弧线转动给人希望，但对于已经太过消极的人而言，这希望太过艰难遥远，不敢企望。自由是一个被回避的梦，如果自由真的能重返，能被赎回，那么，憧憬自由的每个夜晚都承受不了，只有天堂才够宽广，能容纳下自由。

如记忆中还是男孩时——
在水池里泼水——
而不过是一次更娴静的巡回——
一次几何般空洞的①沉醉——

钥匙的姿势
插进白日的闲暇
抵达我们的努力——并未如此逼真
真似那自由的脸颊——

相比于这幻魅的钢——
它的形象——夜夜日日——
出现在眼前——似为我们所有——
也似乎真的——无可逃避——

那狭长的圆圈——那固定的一点——
那缓慢流转的希冀——
对某种更消极的东西而言——其内涵
太深远难以企及——

我们所知的自由
被回避——像一个梦幻——
对于夜晚太过宽广除非是天堂——
如果那——真的——可以重返——

653

Of Being is a Bird
The likest to the Down

---

① 几何般空洞的（Geometric）：*Emily Dickinson Lexicon* 认为诗中"Geometric"有"stinting"和"scanty"之喻。译者认为更有如几何般空洞、空虚之喻，展示了诗中说话者在牢笼里听狱卒的脚步声所感受到的那种快乐的空洞、空虚性质，表明自由是遥遥无期的。

An Easy Breeze do put afloat
The General Heavens—upon—

It soars—and shifts—and whirls—
And measures with the Clouds
In easy—even—dazzling pace—
No different the Birds—

Except a Wake of Music
Accompany their feet—
As did the Down emit a Tune—
For Ecstasy—of it

653
那存在是一只鸟
像极了羽绒
一阵柔和的风
把广袤的天空——轻托在手中——

它从低处蹿起——变向——转圈——
和流云嬉戏
以优雅——平稳——令人眩晕的步伐——
与飞鸟们无异——

除了袅袅乐音
追随它们足迹——
仿佛那羽绒也唱起一支曲儿——
抒发——它的狂喜

654
A long—long Sleep—A famous—Sleep—
That makes no show for Morn—
By Stretch of Limb—or stir of Lid—

An independent One—

Was ever idleness like This?
Upon a Bank of Stone
To bask the Centuries away—
Nor once look up—for Noon?

654

一个长长的——睡眠——一个闻名的——睡眠——
也不起身恭迎清晨——
只伸伸四肢——或眨眨眼皮——
这了无牵挂的人——

有这样懒散的么?
在一堆石头上
晒几世纪的太阳——
甚至不对正午——看上一眼?

655

Without this—there is nought—
All other Riches be
As is the Twitter of a Bird—
Heard opposite the Sea—

I could not care—to gain
A lesser than the Whole—
For did not this include themself—
As Seams—include the Ball?

I wished a way might be
My Heart to subdivide—
'Twould magnify—the Gratitude—
And not reduce—the Gold—

655

没有了这——一切皆空——
所有其他财富
就像鸟的鸣啭——
在大海对岸发出——

我没法在意——所得
少于全部——
难道这不包含它们么——
像秋波——已含眼珠?

我希望能有一个办法
切分我的心——
这样就可以增加——感激——
而不会减少——黄金——

656

The name—of it—is "Autumn"—
The hue—of it—is Blood—
An Artery—upon the Hill—
A Vein—along the Road—

Great Globules—in the Alleys—
And Oh, the Shower of Stain—
When Winds—upset the Basin—
And spill the Scarlet Rain—

It sprinkles Bonnets—far below—
It gathers ruddy Pools—
Then—eddies like a Rose—away—
Upon Vermilion Wheels—

656

它的名字——叫——"秋天"——
它的色彩——是——血红——
一条动脉——现山间——
一条静脉——沿路通——

无数的水滴——洒落街巷——
啊,淅淅沥沥的雨——
当风——吹皱水池——
使深红的雨水流溢——

它撒下无数软帽——在地面——
攒成一个个微红水洼——
然后——玫瑰般旋转——消散——
在朱红的轮子上——

657

I dwell in Possibility—
A fairer House than Prose—
More numerous of Windows—
Superior—for Doors—

Of Chambers as the Cedars—
Impregnable of Eye—
And for an Everlasting Roof
The Gambrels of the Sky—

Of Visitors—the fairest—
For Occupation—This—
The spreading wide my narrow Hands
To gather Paradise—

657
我居住在可能里——
它比散文的房子更美——
窗户更多——
门庭——更宏伟——

房间似雪松——
眼睛看不透——
至于那永恒的屋顶
则是天空的穹窿——

访客——最惬意——
如果住在——这栋房——
张开我小手就可以
触到天堂——

658
Whole Gulfs—of Red, and Fleets—of Red—
And Crews—of solid Blood—
Did place about the West—Tonight—
As 'twere specific Ground—

And They—appointed Creatures—
In Authorized Arrays—
Due—promptly—as a Drama—
That bows—and disappears—

658
一湾湾——红,一队队——红——
还有一块块——血色鲜艳——
都布在西天——今晚——
仿佛别致的地面——

他们——准时出现的生灵——
按规定站好位置——
准时——快捷——像演戏——
躬身谢幕——然后消失——

659

That first Day, when you praised Me, Sweet,
And said that I was strong—
And could be mighty, if I liked—
That Day—the Days among—

Glows Central—like a Jewel
Between Diverging Golds—
The Minor One—that gleamed behind—
And Vaster—of the World's.

659

那头一天,当你赞美我,亲爱的,
说我强壮——
会很有力量,如果我想——
那一天——就熠熠发光——

在诸多日子中——像一颗宝石
在光影迷离的金子间——
这不起眼的一颗——在后面闪亮——
却比全世界的光明——更浩瀚。

660

'Tis good—the looking back on Grief—
To re-endure a Day—
We thought the Mighty Funeral—
Of All Conceived Joy—

To recollect how Busy Grass
Did meddle—one by one—
Till all the Grief with Summer—waved
And none could see the stone.

And though the Wo you have Today
Be larger—As the Sea
Exceeds it's Unremembered Drop—
They're Water—equally—

660

这挺好——回顾悲伤——
重新体验那一日——
我们认为是所有已知欢乐的——
宏大葬礼——

回忆忙碌的小草
如何招摇———棵接一棵①——
直至所有的悲伤随夏日——起伏
没人看见那石头②。

虽然你今日的悲戚
更宽广——似海洋
超过它无人忆念的水滴——
它们③也是水——同样——

661

Could I but ride indefinite

---

① 本行或喻指悲伤的坟头上芳草萋萋。
② 石头（the stone）：或指墓碑。本节可能是描绘了夏日回归时，坟头芳草茂盛，墓碑掩映其中的寂寥凄清场景。
③ 它们（They）：应是指今日的悲伤和过去的悲伤。

As doth the Meadow Bee
And visit only where I liked
And No one visit me

And flirt all Day with Buttercups
And marry whom I may
And dwell a little everywhere
Or better, run away

With no Police to follow
Or chase Him if He do
Till He should jump Peninsulas
To get away from me—

I said "But just to be a Bee"
Upon a Raft of Air
And row in Nowhere all Day long
And anchor "off the Bar"

What Liberty! So Captives deem
Who tight in Dungeons are.

661
我愿能无拘无束地游弋
如草地上的蜜蜂般快活
只造访我喜欢之地
没有谁来造访我

整日与金凤花谈情
与我钟情的对象结成伴侣
四处随意驻停
或最好，翩翩离去

没有警察跟踪
他要跟就干脆对他紧追
直至他跳上半岛
摆脱我的追随——

我说"只要做一只蜜蜂"
在一只空气筏上
整日在乌有乡划着游荡
在"海滩外"① 停航

多么自在啊！那些深陷地牢的俘虏
如此向往。

662

Embarrassment of one another
And God
Is Revelation's limit,
Aloud
Is nothing that is chief,
But still,
Divinity dwells under a seal.

662

互感难堪
上帝
是天谕的局限，
高声
并非重点，
但仍然，
有神性寓居在封条下面。

---

① 海滩外（off the Bar）：据 *Emily Dickinson Lexicon*，bar 有 beach、strand、bank of sand 之意。

663

Again—his voice is at the door—
I feel the old *Degree*—
I hear him ask the servant
For such an one—as me—

I take a *flower*—as I go—
My face to *justify*—
He never *saw* me—*in this life*—
I might *surprise* his eye!

I cross the Hall with *mingled* steps—
I—silent—pass the door—
I look on all this world *contains*—
Just his face—nothing more!

We talk in *careless*—and it toss—
A kind of *plummet* strain—
Each—sounding—shyly—
Just—how—deep—
The *other's* one—had been—

We *walk*—I leave my Dog—at home—
A *tender* — *thoughtful* Moon—
Goes with us—just a little way—
And—then—we are *alone*—

Alone—if Angels are "alone" —
First time they *try* the *sky*!
Alone—if those "vailed faces" —be—
We cannot *count*—on High!

I'd give—to live that hour—*again*—

The purple—*in my Vein*—
But He must *count the drops—himself* —
My price for *every stain*!

663
再一次——他的声音在门口响起——
我又感受那熟悉的深沉——
听到他问仆人
打听像我这样的——一个人——

我带上一枝花——随我出去——
使我的脸更加美丽——
他从未见过我——在如今的生活里——
我恐怕会让他的眼大感惊奇!

快步穿过厅堂——
我——悄悄——经过门口——
搜寻这世界的所有收藏——
除了他的脸——什么都没有!

我们随意交谈——声音忽高忽低——
像骤降的铅锤——
每一声——听起来——羞滴滴——
那——另一位的声音——
曾经——多么——深邃——

我们出去散步——我留下我的狗——在家里——
温柔——体贴的月亮——
与我们相随——但只跟了一会儿——
然后——就——只剩孤单的我俩——

孤单——如果天使们"孤单"——
他们首先会在天上闯荡!

孤单——如果那些"遮掩的脸"——孤单——
我们就无法指望——天堂!

我愿——把那个时辰——重过一遍——
紫色——在我血管里流——
但他一定要亲自数——每一滴——
我会为每一滴付出报酬!

664

Of all the Souls that stand create—
I have elected—One—
When Sense from Spirit—files away—
And Subterfuge—is done—
When that which is—and that which was—
Apart—intrinsic—stand—
And this brief Drama in the flesh—
Is shifted—like a Sand—
When Figures show their royal Front—
And Mists—are carved away,
Behold the Atom—I preferred—
To all the lists of Clay!

664

从神创造的所有灵魂里——
我挑选了——一位——
当感觉从精神——脱离——
骗局——已完备——
当那此在——和曾在——
分开——在内部——独立——
这出肉体的短剧——
轮番上演——像沙粒——
当万物显出高贵的正面——
迷雾——被驱散,

看那细小的一粒——是我所选——
自尘土所有的名单!

665
Dropped into the Ether Acre—
Wearing the Sod Gown—
Bonnet of Everlasting Laces—
Brooch—frozen on—

Horses of Blonde—and Coach of Silver—
Baggage a strapped Pearl—
Journey of Down—and Whip of Diamond—
Riding to meet the Earl—

665
坠入茫茫苍天——
身穿草皮的礼服——
长带飘飘的软帽——
胸针——凝固——

浅黄的马——银白的车——
行李是一颗带条纹的珍珠——
绒毛的旅途——钻石的鞭子——
驱车去见王公贵族——

666
Ah, Teneriffe!
Retreating Mountain!
Purples of Ages—pause for *you*—

Sunset—reviews her Sapphire Regiment—
Day—drops you her Red Adieu!

Still—Clad in your Mail of ices—
Thigh of Granite—and thew—of Steel—
Heedless—alike—of pomp—or parting

Ah, Teneriffe!
I'm kneeling—still—

666①
啊，特纳利夫②！
逐渐退隐的山峰！
经年的紫色——为你停驻——

落日——检阅她蔚蓝的军团——
白昼——为你洒下红色的告别！

而你——依然身披冰的铠甲——
花岗岩的大腿——钢的——筋肉——
对眼前的壮丽——或别离——同样——无动于衷

啊，特纳利夫！
我下跪——依然——

667
Bloom upon the Mountain—stated—
Blameless of a Name—
Efflorescence of a Sunset—
Reproduced—the same—

---

① 这是艾米莉·狄金森1863年写给嫂子苏珊（Susan Huntington Gilbert，即Sue）的诗，有两个版本，这是其中之一。

② 特纳利夫（Teneriffe 或 Tenerife [ˌtenəˈriːf]）：大西洋加那利群岛（Canary Islands）中面积最大、人口最多的岛屿，首府是圣克鲁斯（Santa Cruz de Tenerife）。加那利群岛由七大火山岛屿组成，位于非洲西北海岸之外，属于西班牙的一个自治区。

Seed, had I, my Purple Sowing
Should endow the Day—
Not a Topic of a Twilight—
Show itself away—

Who for tilling—to the Mountain
Come, and disappear—
Whose be Her Renown, or fading,
Witness, is not here—

While I state—the Solemn Petals,
Far as North—and East,
Far as South and West—expanding—
Culminate—in Rest—

And the Mountain to the Evening
Fit His Countenance—
Indicating, by no Muscle—
The Experience—

667①

盛开在山巅——壮丽辉煌——
一个无可诟病的名字——
一个落日的绽放——
也不过——如此——

假如我有，种子，我紫色的播种
会长出白日——
没有一个黄昏的热情——
会散失——

---

① 这是写落日的诗，可参阅有类似主题的第307和308首诗。

是谁为耕耘——到山巅
来了，又不见——
哪一位使她闻名，或消散，
在这里，都没显现——

我说话的此刻——那些庄严的花瓣，
远到北边——和东边，
远到南边和西边——不断扩展——
渐至——安歇——

而山峰把自己的面孔
融进夜色朦胧——
无需肌肉的表情，也可暗示——
那个过程——

668

"Nature" is what we see—
The Hill—the Afternoon—
Squirrel—Eclipse—the Bumble bee—
Nay—Nature is Heaven—
Nature is what we hear—
The Bobolink—the Sea—
Thunder—the Cricket—
Nay—Nature is Harmony—
Nature is what we know—
Yet have no art to say—
So impotent Our Wisdom is
To her Simplicity

668

"自然"是我们所见——
山峰——在下午——
松鼠——阴影——还有大黄蜂——

不——自然是天堂——
自然是我们所闻——
食米鸟——大海——
雷霆——蟋蟀——
不——自然是和声——
自然是我们所知——
却难以言明——
在她的淳朴面前
我们的智慧如此无能

669

No Romance sold unto
Could so enthrall a Man
As the perusal of
His Individual One—
'Tis Fiction's—to dilute to Plausibility
Our Novel—When 'tis small enough
To Credit—'Tis'nt true!

669

市场上售卖的浪漫故事
没一部能把一个男人迷住
如他细读
自己的那一部——
凡是虚构——总要稀释至貌似合理
我们的小说——只要太薄
就足以证明——它不是真![①]

670

One need not be a Chamber—to be Haunted—

---

① 最后三行的意思是：小说稀释现实生活，使之成为虚构，同时貌似合理，但是，如果小说稀释或摊薄现实生活太多，也就说明它不是真实的现实生活。

One need not be a House—
The Brain has Corridors—surpassing
Material Place—

Far safer, of a Midnight Meeting
External Ghost
Than it's interior Confronting—
That Cooler Host.

Far safer, through an Abbey gallop,
The Stones a'chase—
Than Unarmed, one's a'self encounter—
In lonesome Place—

Ourself behind ourself, concealed—
Should startle most—
Assassin hid in our Apartment
Be Horror's least.

The Body—borrows a Revolver—
He bolts the Door—
O'erlooking a superior spectre—
Or More—

670

要碰上闹鬼———一个人不必非得是一个房间——
不必非得是一栋房——
头脑有许多走廊——胜过
现实中的地方——

要安全得多，午夜遇上
外部世界的鬼
相比于在内心撞上——

那更恐怖的一位。

要安全得多,疾穿过大教堂,
被石头追击——
相比于毫无防备,一个人遇见自己——
在偏僻之地——

自己在自己背后,隐藏——
最令人惊吓——
刺客藏在我们寓所
一点也不可怕。

身体——借了一把左轮手枪——
就把房门插闩上锁——
却忽略了一位超级幽灵——
或者更多——

671

She dwelleth in the Ground—
Where Daffodils—abide—
Her Maker—Her Metropolis—
The Universe—Her Maid—

To fetch Her Grace—and Hue—
And Fairness—and Renown—
The Firmament's—To Pluck Her—
And fetch Her Thee—be mine—

671

她寓居在地里——
黄水仙也在那里——停驻——
她的缔造者——是她的大都市——
宇宙——是她的女仆——

带给她荣耀——和色彩——
还有美丽——和声名卓著——
是上苍的工作——而把她①采摘——
将她带给你——是我的任务——

672
The Future—never spoke—
Nor will He—like the Dumb—
Reveal by sign—a syllable
Of His Profound To Come—

But when the News be ripe—
Presents it—in the Act—
Forestalling Preparation—
Escape—or Substitute—

Indifference to Him—
The Dower—as the Doom—
His Office—but to execute
Fate's—Telegram—to Him—

672
未来——从不言语——
也不会——像哑人——
用手势示意——一个音
表明他将大驾光临——

但当消息得到证实——
体现——在事件里——
阻止了准备——

---

① 她（Her）：指番红花（crocus）。这是艾米莉·狄金森1863年写给嫂子苏珊的诗，随诗附有一个说明"With a crocus."（随附一枝番红花）。

逃避——或代替——

也不必对他心惊——
那天降之物——就像注定的噩耗——
他的工作——只是执行
命运——给他的——电报——

673

The Love a Life can show Below
Is but a filament, I know,
Of that diviner thing
That faints upon the face of Noon—
And smites the Tinder in the Sun—
And hinders Gabriel's Wing—

'Tis this—in Music—hints and sways—
And far abroad on Summer days—
Distils uncertain pain—
'Tis this enamors in the East—
And tints the Transit in the West
With harrowing Iodine—

'Tis this—invites—appalls—endows—
Flits—glimmers—proves—dissolves—
Returns—suggests—convicts—enchants—
Then—flings in Paradise—

673

下界的生活能展示的爱
我知道,仅是那更神圣事物的,
一缕一丝
它在正午的脸上渐褪渐浅——
击打太阳的导火线——

阻止加百利天使展翅——

是它——在音乐里——隐示和摇弋——
在外面广阔的夏季——
析出缕缕忐忑——
是它在东方使人神驰——
给西方的交接仪式
涂上凄惨的碘色——

是它——引诱——惊吓——又给予——
飞掠——闪烁——清晰——又消散——
返回——暗示——确定——令人沉迷——
然后——又遁入天堂——

674

The Soul that hath a Guest
Doth seldom go abroad—
Diviner Crowd at Home—
Obliterate the need—

And Courtesy forbid
A Host's departure when
Upon Himself be visiting
The Emperor of Men—

674

有访客的灵魂
确实外出很少——
更神圣的一群在家——
取消了这个需要——

礼节也禁止
主人离开

当人子之王来访
要他接待——

675

Essential Oils—are wrung—
The Attar from the Rose
Be not expressed by Suns—alone—
It is the gift of Screws—

The General Rose—decay—
But this—in Lady's Drawer
Make Summer—When the Lady lie
In Ceaseless Rosemary—

675①

精油——被榨出——
这源自玫瑰的花油
并非仅靠阳光——挤压——
也是榨油机的献赠——

普通的玫瑰——会枯萎——
但这个——收在女士的抽屉
在那位女士躺下时——使夏季
充满迷迭香气——

676

Least Bee that brew—
A Honey's Weight
The Summer multiply—

---

① 艾米莉·狄金森的文学导师希金森在《大西洋月刊》1862 年 4 月号上发表的 "Letter to a Young Contributor" 一文中有这样的说法: "Literature is attar of roses, one distilled drop from a million blossoms." 狄金森读过那篇文章后不久,即向希金森写信请教诗歌问题。

Content Her smallest fraction help
The Amber Quantity—

676①
再小的蜜蜂也会酿蜜——
夏季每增加
一份蜜的重量——
都令她满意她最小的一份
也有益于那琥珀色的数量——

677
To be alive—is Power—
Existence—in itself—
Without a further function—
Omnipotence—Enough—

To be alive—and Will!
'Tis able as a God—
The Maker—of Ourselves—be what—
Such being Finitude!

677②
活着——就是力量——
存在——本身——
不需再做努力——
就足以——无所不能——

---

① 也可译为：再小的蜜蜂酿出——/一份蜜的重量/也能使夏季增长——/很高兴她最小的一份也有益于/那琥珀色的数量——

② 这是艾米莉·狄金森 1863 年（富兰克林版认为是 1864 年）写给她嫂子苏珊的诗。狄金森对人和人间的肯定和赞美，散见于她的诗信中，例如，她在 1870 年写给苏珊的字条中写道："Oh Matchless Earth – We underrate the chance to dwell in Thee."（L347）写于 1877 年的第 1408 首诗中也有："The Fact that Earth is Heaven –/Whether Heaven is Heaven or not"。

活着——并且追求!
可以能干如上帝——
我们的——造物主——也不过——
如此而已!

678

Wolfe demanded during dying
"Which obtain the Day"?
"General, the British" — "Easy"
Answered Wolfe "to die"

Montcalm, his opposing Spirit
Rendered with a smile
"Sweet" said he "my own Surrender
Liberty's beguile"

678①

沃尔夫②临终前问
"那天获胜是哪一边"?
"将军,是英国人"——"这下"

---

① 七年战争(Seven Years' War, 1756—1763)中,欧洲不少国家都被牵涉其中,一方以英国和普鲁士为主要力量,另一方以法国和澳大利亚为主要力量,各列强在欧洲、北美和亚洲等地区展开势力范围的争夺。其中,在 1759 年 9 月 13 日的加拿大魁北克战役(Battle of Quebec, 或 Battle of the Plains of Abraham)中,沃尔夫(James P. Wolfe)将军指挥英军在围困魁北克 3 个月之后,在魁北克城墙外的一片高原上击溃了由蒙特卡姆(Louis Joseph de Montcalm)将军指挥的法国军队防线,攻克了魁北克,两位将军均在战斗中牺牲。魁北克之战对后续加拿大境内的其他战斗影响巨大,同时,此战胜利及沃尔夫将军之死,在英国的历史、文化、艺术中有深远影响。

② 沃尔夫:James P. Wolfe(1727—1759),英国将军。1759 年他指挥英军在进攻魁北克的战斗中击败法国将军蒙特卡姆指挥的法军,在 9 月 13 日当天的激战中身中三弹,不幸牺牲。据说沃尔夫曾在战前对他的军官们背诵英国诗人托马斯·格雷(Thomas Gray, 1716—1771)的长诗 *Elegy Written in a Country Churchyard*(1751),然后说:"Gentlemen, I would rather have written that poem than take Quebec tomorrow."他成为英军在七年之战中英国胜利的象征,被称为"The Hero of Quebec""The Conqueror of Quebec",甚至"The Conqueror of Canada",他的英雄形象更随着著名绘画 *The Death of General Wolfe* 而广为流传。

沃尔夫答"可以放心去了"

蒙特卡姆①,他对面的幽灵
脸上堆出笑的模样
"亲爱的"他说"我自己臣服的
原是自由的假象"②

679

Conscious am I in my Chamber,
Of a shapeless friend—
He doth not attest by Posture—
Nor Confirm—by Word—

Neither Place—need I present Him—
Fitter Courtesy
Hospitable intuition
Of His Company—

Presence—is His furthest license—
Neither He to Me
Nor Myself to Him—by Accent—
Forfeit Probity—

Weariness of Him, were quainter
Than Monotony
Knew a Particle—of Space's

---

① 蒙特卡姆:Louis Joseph de Montcalm (1712—1759),法国将军。他在1759年9月13日的魁北克保卫战中指挥法国军队与英国将军沃尔夫指挥的英军激战,战败撤退时腹部中弹受伤,被送至战地医院。据说当医生告诉他回天乏术时,他很平静地回答:"I am glad of it."他于第二天(9月14日)午夜时分死去,他死时并不知道英国将军沃尔夫已早他一天战死。

② "我"虽然死了,臣服于死神,但"我"向之缴械的对象是自由的假象。"我"并未放弃追求自由,即至死依然是为捍卫自由而死,并未屈服。

Vast Society—

Neither if He visit Other—
Do He dwell—or Nay—know I—
But Instinct esteem Him
Immortality—

679
我意识到在我房间，
有一位无形的友朋——
他不用身姿证实——
也不用语言——确认——

我无须给他——引坐——
这样更显礼数
只需殷勤地直觉
他的陪护——

现身——是他最不可能的事——
不论他对我
或我对他——开口——
就丧失了正直——

厌烦他，会更怪异
胜过乏味单一
如一个粒子——认识
空间中广大的群体——

他是否还拜访别处——
是否留宿——或不住——我均不明白——
但本能总觉得他
永在——

680

Each Life Converges to some Centre—
Expressed—or still—
Exists in every Human Nature
A Goal—

Embodied scarcely to itself—it may be—
Too fair
For Credibility's presumption
To mar—

Adored with caution—as a Brittle Heaven—
To reach
Were hopeless, as the Rainbow's Raiment
To touch—

Yet persevered toward—sure—for the Distance—
How high—
Unto the Saint's slow diligence—
The Sky—

Ungained—it may be—by a Life's low Venture—
But then—
Eternity enable the endeavoring
Again.

680

每个生命都向某个中心汇集——
轰轰烈烈——或静悄悄——
每个人心里
都有个目标——

它几乎不显形——或许——
它太美好
可信的推测
也无法抹掉——

小心仰慕——像对易碎的天堂——
要进入
无望，像彩虹的霓裳
难得一触——

但仍坚持前进——更坚定——向远方——
多么高远——
对圣徒们迟缓的勤奋而言——
那苍天——

一生平凡奋斗——也许——毫无收获——
但是——
永恒会令人振作
再次。

681

Soil of Flint, if steady tilled—
Will refund the Hand—
Seed of Palm, by Lybian Sun
Fructified in Sand—

681

坚硬的土地，若经常耕犁——
会回报手的劳作——
棕榈的种子，受利比亚阳光沐浴
会在沙地结硕果——

682

'Twould ease—a Butterfly—
Elate—a Bee—
Thou'rt neither—
Neither—thy capacity—

But, Blossom, were I,
I would rather be
Thy moment
Than a Bee's Eternity—

Content of fading
Is enough for me—
Fade I unto Divinity—

And Dying—Lifetime—
Ample as the Eye—
Her least attention raise on me—

682①

它能使一只蝴蝶——悠然——
让一只蜜蜂——快意——
而你两者都不是——
两者——都非你力所能及——

但，花儿，假使我是你，

---

① 题解：一朵花可以使蝴蝶感到悠然轻松，使蜜蜂舒畅快意，但"你"既不是蝴蝶也不是蜜蜂，没有能力成为它们。这里是说话者对自己说话，称自己为"你"。接着说话者直接自称为"我"，"我"更愿意像花一样能拥有使蝴蝶和蜜蜂悠然快意的那一刻，这样就感觉自己似乎拥有了神一般的能力，成为神了，虽然那一刻是短暂的，但已感满足。而死亡，在"我"一生里，如广袤的天空，这天空也像天堂或上帝之眼，对我极少关心。换言之，我死后是否能升天堂，上帝恐怕极少关注到我，因此，与其企望如蜜蜂一样的永远（永恒），不如企盼此生能拥有片刻的神性感受。

我宁愿
拥有你那一刻
也不要蜜蜂的永远——

欣然遁逝
对我已然足矣——
遁入神境里——

而死亡——整个一生——①
广袤如那只眼——
对我极少留意——

683
The Soul unto itself
Is an imperial friend—
Or the most agonizing Spy—
An Enemy—could send—

Secure against it's own—
No treason it can fear—
Itself—it's Sovereign—of itself
The Soul should stand in Awe—

683②
灵魂对于它自己
是尊贵的友伴——
或最受煎熬的间谍——
由敌方——派遣——

---

① 或可译为：而垂死的——一生——
② 艾米莉·狄金森在1863年2月写给文学导师希金森的一封信（L280）中附寄了本诗。参见第560首诗的题解。

自身安全有保障——
就不担心谁背叛谁——
它自己——是自己的——君主
灵魂应感敬畏——

684

Best Gains—must have the Losses' Test—
To constitute them—Gains—

684①

最好的收获——必经过失落的考验——
才能称之为——收获——

685

Not "Revelation" —'tis—that waits,
But our unfurnished eyes—

---

① 艾米莉·狄金森在 1863 年 2 月写给文学导师希金森的一封信（L280）中写有这两行诗，也写有第 685 首诗的两行诗，而这封信的开头一句则成为第 560 首诗的第二节。希金森在南北战争（1861—1865）早期是马萨诸塞州第 51 步兵团（the 51st Massachusetts Infantry）的一名上尉（captain），他在 1862 年 8 月的一次战斗中受伤而离开步兵团。伤愈后他被任命为南卡罗来纳州志愿军第 1 步兵军团［1st South Carolina Volunteer Infantry Regiment（Colored）］的上校（colonel）指挥官，于 1862 年 11 月至 1864 年 10 月指挥这支黑人军团参加南北战争。狄金森在 1862 年夏天就期待能见到希金森，如她在 1862 年 7 月写给希金森的信中所言："Because you have much business, beside the growth of me - you will appoint, yourself, how often I shall come - without your inconvenience. And if at any time - you regret you received me, or I prove a different fabric to that you supposed - you must banish me - "（L268）但由于希金森上校当时正在参战和受伤，他们两人并未能谋面。正因为战争使狄金森失去了在 1862 年夏天与希金森会面的机会，所以才有 1863 年 2 月她给希金森信中的这些话："I should have liked to see you, before you became improbable. War feels to me an oblique place - Should there be other Summers, would you perhaps come?"（L280）信中还写有本诗的两行，表明最好的、真正的收获（即会面），需先接受失落的考验（两人已失落了一次 1862 年夏天的见面之约）。

685①

不是"启示"——在——等待，
而是我们未准备好的眼睛——

686

They say that "Time assuages" —
Time never did assuage—
An actual suffering strengthens
As Sinews do, with age—

Time is a Test of Trouble—
But not a Remedy—
If such it prove, it prove too
There was no Malady—

686②

他们说"时间会冲淡"——

---

① 艾米莉·狄金森在 1863 年 2 月写给文学导师希金森的一封信（L280）中写有这两行诗。在这两行诗之前，是这样的话："I was thinking, today – as I noticed, that the 'Supernatural,' was only the Natural, disclosed – "表明狄金森认为所谓超自然，只不过是自然的一部分而已，换言之，超自然就在自然之内，藉由自然揭示。人们总希望在自然中发现自然之外的某种"启示""天启"，其实并没有什么超自然的"天启"在等待着人们去发现，所一直等待的只是人们尚未准备好的眼睛。如果眼睛没有足够的能力或技能，就发现不了超自然，就一直在寻找和等待中。反言之，如果眼睛准备好了，有足够的能力，就可以在自然中发现超自然，而无须一直等待。

② 本诗写于 1863 年（富兰克林版认为是 1864 年）。艾米莉·狄金森在 1866 年 6 月 9 日写给文学导师希金森的信（L319）里提到她想念死去的狗 Carlo，并抄录了本诗的第二节。Carlo 是狄金森父亲爱德华（Edward Dickinson, 1803—1874）1849 年送给她的一只纽芬兰犬（Newfoundland），以陪伴喜欢在林子和野外长时散步的狄金森。狄金森在她一些诗歌中提到过 Carlo 的名字，在她信件中也 13 次提到 Carlo，如狄金森在 1850 年情人节前夕写的信中就提到 Carlo："If it was my Carlo now! The Dog is the noblest work of Art, sir. I may safely say the noblest."（L34） 这封信后来以 "Magnum bonum, harem scarum" 为题发表于艾默斯特学院（Amherst College）的学生杂志 The Indicator 二月号上。她在 1862 年 4 月 25 日写给希金森的信中向对方介绍 Carlo："You ask of my Companions Hills – sir – and the Sundown, and a Dog large as myself, that my Father bought me – "（L261）1866 年 Carlo 死后，狄金森又在 1866 年 1 月末写给希金森的一封短信里说："Carlo died –/E. Dickinson / Would you instruct me now?"（L314）几个月后的 6 月 9 日，她再次写信给希金森，提到 Carlo，并抄录了本诗第二节。

时间从不会冲淡——
真切的痛苦只会增强
像肌腱，随年龄的增长——

时间只验证烦恼——
而非治疗——
如果真能治疗，也就证明
世上没有疾病——

687

I'll send the feather from my Hat!
Who knows—but at the sight of that
My Sovreign will relent?
As trinket—worn by faded Child—
Confronting eyes long—comforted—
Blisters the Adamant!

687①

我会寄出我帽上的羽毛！
谁知道——只需用眼一扫
我的君王就心软？
像小物件——由过世的孩子所佩——
看久了——就感安慰——
磐石也会冒水泡！

688

"*Speech*" —is a prank of *Parliament*—
"*Tears*" —is a trick of the *nerve*—
But the Heart with the heaviest freight on—
Does'nt—always—move—

---

① 这是艾米莉·狄金森1861年写给朋友鲍尔斯（Samuel Bowles, 1826—1878）的诗。

688①
"演说"——是国会里的恶作剧——
"泪水"——是神经玩的把戏——
但心负载了最重的货物——
并不——总能——挪移②——

689

The Zeroes—taught us—Phosphorous—
We learned to like the Fire
By playing Glaciers—when a Boy—
And Tinder—guessed—by power
Of Opposite—to balance Odd—
If White—a Red—must be!
Paralysis—our Primer—dumb—
Unto Vitality!

689

寒冷到零——让我们了解了——磷——
对火学会欢喜
通过砌冰屋游戏——在男孩时期——
而对火绒——猜测——通过它
反面的威力——使单一平衡——
如果有白——就有红——无疑!
瘫痪——我们的雷管——藉由无声——
展现活力!

---

① 本诗是艾米莉·狄金森1862年初写给朋友鲍尔斯的一封信的结尾部分,开头是:"I can't thank you any more – You are thoughtful so many times, you grieve me always – now. The old words are numb – and there a'nt any new ones – Brooks – are useless – in Freshet – time – / When you come to Amherst, please God it were Today – I will tell you about the picture – if I can, I will – "(L252)紧接着便以本诗结尾。

② 挪移(move):move也有感动之意。人有嘴就会说,就能花言巧语;有感情就会动情,就会有泪水,但沉重的心并不总能被感动。

690

Victory comes late—
And is held low to freezing lips—
Too rapt with frost
To take it—
How sweet it would have tasted—
Just a Drop—
Was God so economical?
His Table's spread too high for Us—
Unless We dine on tiptoe—
Crumbs—fit such little mouths—
Cherries—suit Robbins—
The Eagle's Golden Breakfast strangles—Them—
God keep His Oath to Sparrows—
Who of little Love—know how to starve—

690①

胜利姗姗来迟——
被低低呈至渐渐冻僵的唇际——
可深恋白霜的双唇
已无法领受——
尝下它该多甜——
哪怕一滴——
难道上帝如此节俭？
他桌上的佳肴太高——
除非我们踮起脚——
面包屑——适合这些小嘴——
樱桃——适合知更鸟——
老鹰金色的早餐会噎死——他们——
上帝信守对麻雀的誓言——

---

① 本诗写于 1863 年（富兰克林版认为是 1861 年）。但狄金森在 1861 年把与本诗只差异 5 个词的一首诗作为一封信（L257）寄给朋友鲍尔斯。

缺少爱怜的麻雀——知道如何捱过饥饿——①

691

Would you like summer? Taste of ours.
Spices? Buy here!
Ill! We have berries, for the parching!
Weary! Furloughs of down!
Perplexed! Estates of violet trouble ne'er looked on!
Captive! We bring reprieve of roses!
Fainting! Flasks of air!
Even for Death, a fairy medicine.
But, which is it, sir?

691②

你会喜欢夏季吗？尝尝我们的。
香料？这里买！
难受！我们有草莓，可解焦渴！
累了！在羽绒上休息！
茫然！大片紫罗兰可保无虞！
被困住！我们用玫瑰暂缓！
晕眩！有长颈瓶里的空气！
即便对于死，也有仙药。
但是，你要哪一个，先生？

---

① 本行也可以译为：麻雀对那些许的爱——知道如何渴望——（即 Who [Sparrows] know how to starve of little Love）关于上帝对麻雀的誓言，或可参见英文钦定版《圣经·新约·马太福音》第6章第26节："Behold the fowls of the air: for they sow not, neither do they reap, nor gather into barns; yet your heavenly Father feedeth them. Are ye not much better than they?"（Matthew 6: 26）以及第10章第29节："Are not two sparrows sold for a farthing? and one of them shall not fall on the ground without your Father."（Matthew 10: 29）

② 本诗是艾米莉·狄金森写给病中的朋友鲍尔斯的一封信（L229）的结尾，诗的前面部分是："We hope our joy to see you – gave of it's own degree – to you – We pray for your new health – the prayer that goes not down – when they shut the church – We offer you our cups – stintless – as to the Bee – the Lily, her new Liquors –".信中的"We"指狄金森自己、她的妹妹维尼（Vinnie, 即 Lavinia Norcross Dickinson, 1833—1899）和她的嫂子苏珊。约翰逊根据笔迹推测该信写于1863年（富兰克林版认为是1862年）。

692

The Sun kept setting—setting—still
No Hue of Afternoon—
Upon the Village I perceived—
From House to House 'twas Noon—

The Dusk kept dropping—dropping—still
No Dew upon the Grass—
But only on my Forehead stopped—
And wandered in my Face—

My Feet kept drowsing—drowsing—still
My fingers were awake—
Yet why so little sound—Myself
Unto my Seeming—make?

How well I knew the Light before—
I could not see it now—
'Tis Dying—I am doing—but
I'm not afraid to know—

692

太阳不断下降——下降——静悄悄
没有一丝午后的迷雾——
把我眼中的村庄笼罩——
一屋连着一屋都是正午——

黄昏不断掉落——掉落——静悄悄
草地上没一滴露珠——
只在我额前驻停——
在我脸上踟蹰——

我的脚越来越昏沉——昏沉——静悄悄
我的手指依然灵敏——

但为何——我自己
对恍惚的我——几乎发不出声音?

从前我多么熟悉光——
现在已无法看到——
这是死亡——我正经历——但
我不怕知道——

693

Shells from the Coast mistaking—
I cherished them for All—
Happening in After Ages
To entertain a Pearl—

Wherefore so late—I murmured—
My need of Thee—be done—
Therefore—the Pearl responded—
My Period begin

693①

在海边误拿了一些贝壳——
我对它们精心呵护——
碰巧在多年后
养出了一颗珍珠——

为何这么迟——我自说自话——
我对你的需求——已经截止——
既然如此——珍珠回答——
我的需求从现在开始

694

The Heaven vests for Each

---

① 参见第 452 首诗,也提到珍珠。

In that small Deity
It craved the grace to worship
Some bashful Summer's Day—

Half shrinking from the Glory
It importuned to see
Till these faint Tabernacles drop
In full Eternity—

How imminent the Venture—
As one should sue a Star—
For His mean sake to leave the Row
And entertain Despair—

A Clemency so common—
We almost cease to fear—
Enabling the minutest—
And furthest—to adore—

694①
上苍赐予每个事物
那小小的神灵
它渴望有幸仰慕
某个羞怯的夏日——

面对荣耀却畏缩不前
虽然它渴求一见

---

① 题解：上苍赋予万物灵性，或形象地说，万物身上都有一个小神灵。万物的灵渴望得到恩典（Grace），能有幸仰慕某个夏日。它虽然一直盼得天恩，强求一见夏日，但真面对这个荣耀（Glory）时，却畏缩不前，一直等到万物的躯壳枯萎，遁入永恒之中。这事情（荣耀）很快就会出现，正如有人请求星星为不起眼的因由来宽慰自己的绝望那样，很快就会有回应。上苍的这种仁慈如此常见，使我们对上苍不再心怀恐惧，那再小再遥远的事物，也会对上苍心生敬慕。本诗可能写的是夏日与上苍的关系，即夏日隐现了上苍存在的影子，包括上苍的仁慈。

直至这些虚弱的躯壳①
都坠入茫茫的永远——

这事情近在眉睫——
正如某个人恳请星星帮忙——
为他卑微的理由离开队列②
去宽慰绝望——

如此平常的仁慈情愫——
让我们几乎不再恐怖——
也使那些最细小的——
和最遥远的事物——心生敬慕——

695

As if the Sea should part
And show a further Sea—
And that—a further—and the Three
But a presumption be—

Of Periods of Seas—
Unvisited of Shores—
Themselves the Verge of Seas to be—
Eternity—is Those—

695

仿佛大海要分开
以展示一片更宽阔的海——
然后——再分开——展示第三片海
但这只是瞎猜——

在海的各个阶段——

---

① 躯壳（Tabernacle）：原指帐篷、临时房屋、礼拜堂、神龛等，这里应是指万物（包括生命）寓居的躯壳。
② 队列（Row）：也可指"吵闹"。

那些人迹未至的海岸——
就是海的边缘——
所谓永恒——就是那些——

696

Their Height in Heaven comforts not—
Their Glory—nought to me—
'Twas best imperfect—as it was—
I'm finite—I can't see—

The House of Supposition—
The Glimmering Frontier that
Skirts the Acres of Perhaps—
To Me—shows insecure—

The Wealth I had—contented me—
If 'twas a meaner size—
Then I had counted it until
It pleased my narrow Eyes—

Better than larger values—
That show however true—
This timid life of Evidence
Keeps pleading—"I don't know."

696

他们在高高的天堂也未心安——
他们的荣耀——我一点也不想念——
这是最大的缺憾——一如从前——
我的生命有限——我看不见——

那假设的房屋——
那闪烁的远方
围起一片想象的疆土——

对我来说——都靠不住——

我所拥有的财富——已令我满足——
假如它价值较低——
我会一直计数
直至令我眯长的眼睛满意——

胜过那更大的价值——
不论有多真实——
这卑微而真确的生命
不断地辩白——"我不知。"

697

I could bring You Jewels—had I a mind to—
But You have enough—of those—
I could bring You Odors from St. Domingo—
Colors—from Vera Cruz—

Berries of the Bahamas—have I—
But this little Blaze
Flickering to itself—in the Meadow—
Suits Me—more than those—

Never a Fellow matched this Topaz—
And his Emerald Swing—
Dower itself—for Bobadilo—
Better—Could I bring?

697①

我可以带珠宝给你——如果我有意——

---

① 艾米莉·狄金森的哥哥威廉·奥斯汀·狄金森（William Austin Dickinson, 1829—1895）的情人托德夫人（Mabel Loomis Todd, 1856—1932）誊抄了本诗的原稿，并附注："随附凤仙花。"（"With jewelweed."）若果真如此，则诗中的"这一小块发光物体"（this little Blaze）和"黄玉"（Topaz）或是指凤仙花。

但你已够多——那些东西——
我可以带圣多明各①的香水给你——
还有维拉克鲁斯②的——花衣——

巴哈马③的浆果——我有——
但这一小块发光物体
在草丛里——闪闪幽幽——
它更适合我——相比其他东西——

没有哪个小伙配得上这块黄玉——
还有它闪烁的翠绿光彩——
这是波巴迪罗④的——嫁妆——
我还能有更好的——带来?

698

Life—is what we make it—
Death—we do not know—
Christ's acquaintance with Him
Justify Him—though—

He—would trust no stranger—
Other—could betray—
Just His own endorsement—

---

① 圣多明各(St. Domingo):加勒比海岛屿。在狄金森的诗信中,St. Domingo 往往指富有蝴蝶、花果和芳馨的热带之地。
② 维拉克鲁斯(Vera Cruz):墨西哥东部墨西哥湾一海港城市,是墨西哥与欧洲贸易的中心海港。
③ 巴哈马(Bahamas):即拉丁美洲国家巴哈马群岛。
④ 波巴迪罗(Bobadilo):中美洲国家萨尔瓦多(El Salvador)西海岸一城镇;西班牙一村庄名;也可能指西班牙征服者和殖民统治者波巴迪拉(Francisco de Bobadilla, 1450—1502),他 1499 年被西班牙费迪南国王(King Ferdinand, 1452—1516)任命为西印度群岛总督(Governor of the Indies, 1499—1502),他在 1500 年抵达加勒比海伊斯帕尼奥拉岛(Hispaniola)的圣多明各殖民地(Colony of Santo Domingo),不久,即指控前任总督、发现美洲大陆的哥伦布(Christopher Columbus, 1451—1506, 1492—1499 任西印度群岛总督)管理不善等罪名,并将哥伦布铐上锁链,遭送回西班牙。

That—sufficeth Me—

All the other Distance
He hath traversed first—
No New Mile remaineth—
Far as Paradise—

His sure foot preceding—
Tender Pioneer—
Base must be the Coward
Dare not venture—now—

698
生活——由我们创造——
死亡——我们不知——
而基督与他熟悉
就证明——他真实——

他——不信任生人——
他人——会背信——
唯有他亲自认可——
那——我才放心——

所有其他地方
他已事先去闯——
无处不曾涉足——
即使远如天堂——

前方是他坚定的脚步——
这温柔的开拓者——
卑鄙属于懦夫
仍不敢尝试——此刻——

699

The Judge is like the Owl—
I've heard my Father tell—
And Owls do build in Oaks—
So here's an Amber Sill—

That slanted in my Path—
When going to the Barn—
And if it serve You for a House—
Itself is not in vain—

About the price—'tis small—
I only ask a Tune
At Midnight—Let the Owl select
His favorite Refrain.

699

法官就像枭——
我曾听父亲讲——
而枭在橡树上筑巢——
这就有一根琥珀色的木梁①——

斜横在我的路上——
当我去往谷仓——
如果它是你的温房——
它就不算白长——

至于说到价格——那并不算高——
我只需一支乐曲
在午夜——枭可以选唱
它最爱的叠句。

---

① 木梁（Sill）：sill 有窗台、门槛、基石之意。另据 *Emily Dickinson Lexicon*，sill 也有 arm、tree branch、base for a bird's nest 之意。

700
You've seen Balloons set—Have'nt You?
So stately they ascend—
It is as Swans—discarded You,
For Duties Diamond—

Their Liquid Feet go softly out
Upon a Sea of Blonde—
They spurn the Air, as 'twere too mean
For Creatures so renowned—

Their Ribbons just beyond the eye—
They struggle—some—for Breath—
And yet the Crowd applaud, below—
They would not encore—Death—

The Gilded Creature strains—and spins—
Trips frantic in a Tree—
Tears open her imperial Veins—
And tumbles in the Sea—

The Crowd—retire with an Oath—
The Dust in Streets—go down—
And Clerks in Counting Rooms
Observe— "'Twas only a Balloon" —

700
你见过放飞的气球——不是吗?
它们如此壮观地升起——
好似天鹅——抛下你,
为了钻石般的大义——

它们清澈的双足轻轻迈出
在金色的海洋漫步——

它们鄙视空气,认为它地位太低
不配如此闻名的尤物——

它们的系带刚到视线以外——
就挣扎着——有点——为呼吸——
而下面的人群,却喝彩——
它们不会再来一遍——死去——

那金色的尤物紧张——晕眩——
慌乱中绊倒在一棵树上——
撕破了它尊贵的皮囊——
跌入海洋——

人群——咒骂着离去——
街上的尘埃——落地——
账房里的伙计
说——"不过是个气球而已"——

701

A Thought went up my mind today—
That I have had before—
But did not finish—some way back—
I could not fix the Year—

Nor where it went—nor why it came
The second time to me—
Nor definitely, what it was—
Have I the Art to say—

But somewhere—in my Soul—I know—
I've met the Thing before—
It just reminded me—'twas all—
And came my way no more—

701

今天我脑里涌起一个想法——
过往它曾出现——
但尚未完全——回首看——
我不能肯定在哪一年——

也不知它消失何处——又来为何故
这第二次降临——
我也不确定,它是何物——
我无法说清——

但在我灵魂——某处——我知道——
我曾邂逅这东西——
它仅令我想起——如此而已——
过后再没来袭——

702

A first Mute Coming—
In the Stranger's House—
A first fair Going—
When the Bells rejoice—

A first Exchange—of
What hath mingled—been—
For Lot—exhibited to
Faith—alone—

702

初次悄悄地到来——
在那陌生人的屋房——
初次平静地离开——
当钟声将欢乐敲响——

初次交换——那

已混合的——东西——
因为罗得①——显示了
信仰——独自——

703

Out of sight? What of that?
See the Bird—reach it!
Curve by Curve—Sweep by Sweep—
Round the Steep Air—
Danger! What is that to Her?
Better 'tis to fail—there—
Than debate—here—

Blue is Blue—the World through—
Amber—Amber—Dew—Dew—
Seek—Friend—and see—
Heaven is shy of Earth—that's all—
Bashful Heaven—thy Lovers small—
Hide—too—from thee—

703②

在视线以远？那算啥？
看那只鸟——追上它！
拐弯再拐弯——飞掠又飞掠——
围绕湍急的大气——
危险！那对她算啥？

---

① 罗得（Lot）：英文钦定版《圣经·旧约·创世纪》第19章记载，两位天使来到所多玛城（Sodom），受到罗得的热情款待，天使告诉罗得说上帝要毁灭所多玛城和蛾摩拉城（Gomorrah），敦促罗得携妻子和两个女儿赶快逃出所多玛城，离开平原地带，往山区避难，逃跑过程中不得回头看。罗得离开所多玛城后，天亮了，太阳出来了，这时上帝撒下硫磺与火，毁灭了所多玛城和蛾摩拉城，跑在后边的罗得妻子不禁回头看，就变成了一根盐柱（But his wife looked back from behind him, and she became a pillar of salt.）（Genesis 19：26）。

② 题解：天堂在视线以外，但要有勇气追寻，像鸟儿，就追上了天堂。人间和天堂都是一样的世界，同样有蔚蓝、琥珀黄和露珠。如果你去追寻，去找寻友伴，就会发现，原来只是天堂和人间互相羞怯地躲着对方，所以互相看不见，这就是奥妙所在。

在那里——失败——
胜过空谈——在此地——

蔚蓝仍是蔚蓝——满世界到处——
琥珀——还是琥珀——露珠——还是露珠——
找寻——友伴——会发现——
天堂羞见大地——就这点奥妙——
羞怯的天堂——你那些爱慕者渺小——
同样——对你——躲闪——

704

No matter—now—Sweet—
But when I'm Earl—
Wont you wish you'd spoken
To that dull Girl?

Trivial a Word—just—
Trivial—a Smile—
But wont you wish you'd spared one
When I'm Earl?

I shant need it—then—
Crests—will do—
Eagles on my Buckles—
On my Belt—too—

Ermine—my familiar Gown—
Say—Sweet—then
Wont you wish you'd smiled—just—
Me upon?

704

现在——无关紧要——亲爱的——
但到我贵为伯爵的未来——

你不希望你曾攀谈
那位无趣的女孩?

仅仅——一句微言——
轻轻——一个微笑——
但你不希望你曾将一个人宽恕
当我享有伯爵荣耀?

我不需要这些——到时——
有羽饰——就足够——
有鹰印在我搭扣——
腰带上——也有——

貂皮——是家常衣——
说吧——亲爱的——到那时
你不希望你曾——只——
对我笑?

705

Suspense—is Hostiler than Death—
Death—thosoever Broad,
Is Just Death, and cannot increase—
Suspense—does not conclude—

But perishes—to live anew—
But just anew to die—
Annihilation—plated fresh
With Immortality—

705

悬念——比死亡更有敌意——
死亡——不论含义多丰富,
也就是死亡,不会增加——
悬念——则远未结束——

而是消逝——复活——
又再次死亡——
这种毁灭——每次都镀上
永生的光芒——

706

Life, and Death, and Giants—
Such as These—are still—
Minor—Apparatus—Hopper of the Mill—
Beetle at the Candle—
Or a Fife's Fame—
Maintain—by Accident that they proclaim—

706

生命,死亡,巨人——
诸如这些——已然静默——
较小的——物件——磨坊的料斗——
蜡烛上的甲虫——
或横笛的声名——
则依然故我——根据他们公布的动静——

707

The Grace—Myself—might not obtain—
Confer upon My flower—
Refracted but a Countenance—
For I—inhabit Her—

707

上天的恩典——我自己——恐难得到——
就请授给我的花朵——
它像一张脸庞闪烁——
因为那里——是我的寓所——

708

I sometimes drop it, for a Quick—
The Thought to be alive—
Anonymous Delight to know—
And Madder—to concieve—

Consoles a Wo so monstrous
That did it tear all Day,
Without an instant's Respite—
'Twould look too far—to Die—

Delirium—diverts the Wretch
For Whom the Scaffold neighs—
The Hammock's Motion lulls the Heads
So close on Paradise—

A Reef—crawled easy from the Sea
Eats off the Brittle Line—
The Sailor does'nt know the Stroke—
Until He's past the Pain—

708

我有时放下它，为了生存——
那还活着的思想——
知道已感无名的快乐——
憧憬——就更疯狂——

安慰如此巨大的悲伤
它使人整日泪水涟涟，
没一刻停缓——
看来离消失——还远——

谵妄——让不幸者麻木
绞刑架为他嘶鸣哀伤——

吊索的摆动使头颅迷糊
如此接近天堂——

一座暗礁——悄悄爬出海面
吞食了易碎的航线——
水手没意识到撞击——
直至他的悲痛消散——

709
Publication—is the Auction
Of the Mind of Man—
Poverty—be justifying
For so foul a thing

Possibly—but We—would rather
From Our Garret go
White—Unto the White Creator—
Than invest—Our Snow—

Thought belong to Him who gave it—
Then—to Him Who bear
Its Corporeal illustration—Sell
The Royal Air—

In the Parcel—Be the Merchant
Of the Heavenly Grace—
But reduce no Human Spirit
To Disgrace of Price—

709
发表——是一种拍卖
对人的心灵——
贫穷——认为合理
做这卑鄙的事情

或许——但我们——更愿意
从我们的阁楼辞世
一尘不染——到白色的造物主那里——
也不用我们的雪白——投资——

思想属于给予者——
然后——才属于携带者自己
它有形的躯壳——应该卖给
高贵的空气——

包在包裹里——假如是商人
贩卖上天的荣誉——
但别让人类的心灵蒙受
价格的鄙夷——

710

The Sunrise runs for Both—
The East—Her Purple Troth
Keeps with the Hill—
The Noon unwinds Her Blue
Till One Breadth cover Two—
Remotest—still—

Nor does the Night forget
A Lamp for Each—to set—
Wicks wide away—
The North—Her blazing Sign
Erects in Iodine—
Till Both—can see—

The Midnight's Dusky Arms
Clasp Hemispheres, and Homes
And so
Upon Her Bosom—One—

And One upon Her Hem—
Both lie—

710
日出为那两位而出现——
东方——它紫色的誓言
洒在群山间——
正午展开它的蔚蓝
一口气将那两位遮掩——
它们——依然杳远——

夜晚也不会遗忘
把它们各自的灯盏——点上——
灯芯宽广无边——
北方——闪闪熠熠
屹立在苍茫紫色里——
直到那两位——都看见——

午夜昏暗的手臂
把半个地球,和家园拥在怀里
所以
一位——在它胸前——
另一位在它裙边——
都已躺下歇息——

711
Strong Draughts of Their Refreshing Minds
To drink—enables Mine
Through Desert or the Wilderness
As bore it Sealed Wine—

To go elastic—Or as One
The Camel's trait—attained—
How powerful the Stimulus
Of an Hermetic Mind—

711①

他们清新思想的醇香
饮下——能令我的思想
穿越沙漠或蛮荒
仿佛携着密封的佳酿——

欢快前行——或者像
获得了——骆驼的特长——
多么强大的激励
一个隐秘的思想——

712

Because I could not stop for Death—
He kindly stopped for me—
The Carriage held but just Ourselves—
And Immortality.

We slowly drove—He knew no haste
And I had put away
My labor and my leisure too,
For His Civility—

We passed the School, where Children strove
At Recess—in the Ring—
We passed the Fields of Gazing Grain—
We passed the Setting Sun—

Or rather—He passed Us—
The Dews drew quivering and chill—
For only Gossamer, my Gown—
My Tippet—only Tulle—

---

① 参见第1587首，主题类似。

We paused before a House that seemed
A Swelling of the Ground—
The Roof was scarcely visible—
The Cornice—in the Ground—

Since then—'tis Centuries—and yet
Feels shorter than the Day
I first surmised the Horses' Heads
Were toward Eternity—

712
因为我不能停步等候死神——
他殷勤停车等我——
马车里乘载的只有我俩——
还有永生同座。

我们缓慢行驶——他知无须着急
我也放弃
我的闲暇和操劳，
以回报他的礼貌——

我们经过学校，正逢课间休息
孩童们嬉戏——在操场——
我们经过谷物注目的田野——
我们经过沉落的太阳——

或者说——是他经过我们——
露水令人寒冷和颤抖——
我的外套，只是薄纱——
我的披肩——只是丝绸——

我们在一所房前停下
它像地面的一个隆起——

屋顶几乎不见——
屋檐——陷在地里——

从那时起——已过了几世纪——然而
感觉短过那一天
我那天第一次猜测马头
朝向永远——

713

Fame of Myself, to justify,
All other Plaudit be
Superfluous—An Incense
Beyond Necessity—

Fame of Myself to lack—Although
My Name be else Supreme—
This were an Honor honorless—
A futile Diadem—

713

如果我有声名,是凭真本领,
其他人叫好
就显多余——这种奉承
没必要——

如果我缺乏声名——即使
我的名字可能高贵到顶点——
也只是一项没有荣誉感的荣誉——
一顶无用的冠冕——

714

Rest at Night
The Sun from shining,

Nature—and some Men—
Rest at Noon—some Men—
While Nature
And the Sun—go on—

714①
在夜里歇息
太阳不再照耀，
大自然——和一些人——
而一些人——则在正午歇息——
当大自然
和太阳——还在运转——

715
The World—feels Dusty
When We stop to Die—
We want the Dew—then—
Honors—taste dry—

Flags—vex a Dying face—
But the least Fan
Stirred by a friend's Hand—
Cools—like the Rain—

Mine be the Ministry
When thy Thirst comes—
And Hybla Balms—
Dews of Thessaly, to fetch—

715
世界——感觉尘土仆仆

---

① 题解：在夜里，太阳、大自然，还有一些人都歇息。但有一些人，在大自然和太阳还在运行时，他们就歇息了（逝世了）。

当我们停下来死去——
此时——我们只需甘露——
荣誉——不值一提——

旗帜——让一张垂死的脸气恼——
但扇子摆动微微
由一位友人的手轻摇——
带来清凉——像雨水——

我这里是供给部
当你口渴难熬——
就给你找来，塞萨利①的甘露——
还有希布拉②的香膏——

716

The Day undressed—Herself—
Her Garter—was of Gold—
Her Petticoat—of Purple plain—
Her Dimities—as old

Exactly—as the World—
And yet the newest Star—
Enrolled upon the Hemisphere
Be wrinkled—much as Her—

Too near to God—to pray—
Too near to Heaven—to fear—
The Lady of the Occident
Retired without a care—

---

① 塞萨利（Thessaly）：亦译作"色萨利"，希腊地名。在《圣经》中，是帖撒罗尼迦人（Thessalonians）的聚居地。其在荷马史诗《奥德赛》（*Odyssey*）中以 Aeolia 的名字出现。

② 希布拉（Hybla）：意大利西西里一古代城镇名，位于埃特纳山（Mount Etna）南麓，在古代以盛产蜜而闻名。其位置约在今意大利的帕泰尔诺（Paterno）附近。

Her Candle so expire
The flickering be seen
On Ball of Mast in Bosporus—
And Dome—and Window Pane—

716

白日给自己——卸妆——
她的吊袜带——金色——
她的衬裙——纯紫——
她的细纹上衣——老旧的色泽

完全——似世界的模样——
而那最新一颗星——
出现在天上
也有皱纹——像极她情形——

太近上帝——不必祈祷——
太近天堂——不会恐惧——
那位西方女士
悠然隐去——

她的蜡烛将灭
忽隐忽现
在博斯普鲁斯海峡①的桅杆尖——
在圆屋顶——在窗户边——

717

The Beggar Lad—dies early—
It's Somewhat in the Cold—
And Somewhat in the Trudging feet—

---

① 博斯普鲁斯海峡（Bosporus）：连接黑海和马尔马拉海（Sea of Marmara）的狭长水道，长约30千米（19英里），和达达尼尔海峡（Dardanelles，65千米）一道，成为连接黑海和地中海的重要水上通道。两个海峡均在土耳其境内，将土耳其领土分割成亚洲和欧洲两部分。

And haply, in the World—

The Cruel—smiling—bowing World—
That took its Cambric Way—
Nor heard the timid cry for "Bread"—
"Sweet Lady—Charity"—

Among Redeemed Children
If Trudging feet may stand—
The Barefoot time forgotten—so—
The Sleet—the bitter Wind—

The Childish Hands that teased for Pence
Lifted adoring—then—
To Him whom never Ragged—Coat
Did supplicate in vain—

717
那乞讨的男孩——死得早——
好像在冷天——
好像在跋涉的路上——
或许，在人世间——

那冷酷——微笑——鞠躬的人世间——
遵循彬彬有礼①的方式——
听不见乞求"面包"的怯弱叫喊——
还有"亲爱的女士——发发仁慈"——

如果能站在被救赎的孩子中间
那跋涉的双足——
会忘记过往赤脚时光——完全——

---

① "Cambric"原意为麻纱、细棉布、细亚麻布。*Emily Dickinson Lexicon* 指出其可比喻为 smooth、genteel、polite。

还有冻雨——以及寒风刺骨——

那乞求零钱的稚嫩的手
会向他伸出——满怀敬慕——
对褴褛衣衫的——恳求
他从来都会满足——

718

I meant to find Her when I came—
Death—had the same design—
But the Success—was His—it seems—
And the Surrender—Mine—

I meant to tell Her how I longed
For just this single time—
But Death had told Her so the first—
And she had past, with Him—

To wander—now—is my Repose—
To rest—To rest would be
A privilege of Hurricane
To Memory—and Me.

718①

我来是为找到她——
死神——也有同样计划——
但成功的——是他——好像——
而我——只有投降——

我本想告诉她我多渴望
渴望这一时辰——
但死神抢先告诉了她——

---

① 参见第 58 和 205 首诗与死亡有关的别离主题。

她已离去,跟死神——

漂泊——如今——是我平息的方式——
停下——停下将是
飓风的特权
对于我——和记忆①。

719
A South Wind—has a pathos
Of individual Voice—
As One detect on Landings
An Emigrant's address.

A Hint of Ports and Peoples—
And much not understood—
The fairer—for the farness—
And for the foreignhood.

719
一阵南风——夹着
人声的悲怆——
像一个人在码头
探到移民的去向。

这是港口和人迹的暗示——
但往往不被领会——
它越渺远——越奇异——
就越令人迷醉。

720
No Prisoner be—

---

① 现在,漂泊漫游成了我获得安宁的方式,无法停歇,除非飓风把我和我的记忆扫荡一空,我就不会再想起那被死神带走的"她"了。

Where Liberty—
Himself—abide with Thee—

720
不会有牢囚幽闭——
在自由他自己——
与你同在——之地——

721
Behind Me—dips Eternity—
Before Me—Immortality—
Myself—the Term between—
Death but the Drift of Eastern Gray,
Dissolving into Dawn away,
Before the West begin—

'Tis Kingdoms—afterward—they say—
In perfect—pauseless Monarchy—
Whose Prince—is Son of None—
Himself—His Dateless Dynasty—
Himself—Himself diversify—
In Duplicate divine—

'Tis Miracle before Me—then—
'Tis Miracle behind—between—
A Crescent in the Sea—
With Midnight to the North of Her—
And Midnight to the South of Her—
And Maelstrom—in the Sky—

721
身后——浸染着永恒——
身前——是永生——
我自己——夹在中间——
死神只是东方泛白的流云,

渐渐在拂晓中消散，
在西方肇始之前——

这是王国——随后——他们说——
在这完美——连续的君主国——
王子——是虚无的后裔——
他自己——就是经年的王朝——
他自己——不断变换自己——
以重复的神圣面貌——

所以——我身前是奇迹——
身后也是奇迹——夹击——
一弯新月在海面——
她的北边是午夜——
南边也是午夜——
天上——云舒云卷——

722

Sweet Mountains—Ye tell Me no lie—
Never deny Me—Never fly—
Those same unvarying Eyes
Turn on Me—when I fail—or feign,
Or take the Royal names in vain—
Their far—slow—Violet Gaze—

My Strong Madonnas—Cherish still—
The Wayward Nun—beneath the Hill—
Whose service—is to You—
Her latest Worship—When the Day
Fades from the Firmament away—
To lift Her Brows on You—

722

美丽的群山——你们从不对我说谎——
从不拒绝我——从不飞翔——

那些始终如一的眼目
转向我——当我失意——或佯装如此,
或徒然手握那些高贵的名字——
他们远远——缓缓——紫罗兰般的凝目——

我强健的圣母玛利亚——珍爱有加——
那任性的修女——就在山下——
她的弥撒——是为你——
她最近一次礼拜——当白昼
自天空流走——
是为抬起眼眉能看到你——

723

It tossed—and tossed—
A little Brig I knew—o'ertook by Blast—
It spun—and spun—
And groped delirious, for Morn—

It slipped—and slipped—
As One that drunken—stept—
It's white foot tripped—
Then dropped from sight—

Ah, Brig—Good Night
To Crew and You—
The Ocean's Heart too smooth—too Blue—
To break for You—

723

它颠簸——颠簸——
我认识的一艘小双桅船——被风浪折磨——
它旋转——旋转——
狂乱地寻找,黎明的出现——

它踉跄——踉跄——

像个醉汉——向前闯——
它白色的足跌倒——
就再也看不到——

啊,双桅船——晚安
对你和船员——
大海的心太定——太蓝——
不会为你碎散——

724

It's easy to invent a Life—
God does it—every Day—
Creation—but the Gambol
Of His Authority—

It's easy to efface it—
The thrifty Deity
Could scarce afford Eternity
To Spontaneity—

The Perished Patterns murmur—
But His Perturbless Plan
Proceed—inserting Here—a Sun—
There—leaving out a Man—

724

发明一个生命很容易——
上帝在做——每天——
创造——只是嬉戏
对于他的威权——

要除掉它也容易——
这节俭的神灵
几乎不可能将永恒
赋予这自发的行径——

那些消亡的躯壳低声嚷——
但他的计划有条不紊
继续——这里——安插一个太阳——
那里——省略一个人——

725

Where Thou art—that—is Home—
Cashmere—or Calvary—the same—
Degree—or Shame—
I scarce esteem Location's Name—
So I may Come—

What Thou dost—is Delight—
Bondage as Play—be sweet—
Imprisonment—Content—
And Sentence—Sacrament—
Just We two—meet—

Where Thou art not—is Woe—
Tho' Bands of Spices—row—
What Thou dost not—Despair—
Tho' Gabriel—praise me—Sire—

725

你在哪里——哪里——就是家——
克什米尔①——或耶稣受难地——不必管它——
无论高贵——或卑下——
我几乎不在意住所的名字是否豪华——
所以我会去住下——

---

① 克什米尔（Cashmere）：有两个意思，一指克什米尔地区产的山羊绒（或称开司米羊毛）；一指喜马拉雅山南麓的印度与巴基斯坦争议地区——克什米尔地区（Kashmir）。在狄金森的诗中，"Cashmere"可以喻指天堂乐土或东方亚热带花园。她在第315和726封信中也有提到"Cashmere"。

你所做的——快乐无比——
束缚似游戏般——甜蜜——
禁闭——也令人满意——
判刑——如圣餐礼——
只要我俩——相遇——

你所不在的地方——皆是痛苦——
虽然浓郁的芬芳——遍布——
你所不做之事——令人欲做不能——
虽然加百利天使——表扬我——先生——

726

We thirst at first—'tis Nature's Act—
And later—when we die—
A little Water supplicate—
Of fingers going by—

It intimates the finer want—
Whose adequate supply
Is that Great Water in the West—
Termed Immortality—

726

最初我们口渴——是自然的行为——
后来——当我们辞世——
恳求些许水——
向经过的手指——

它暗示更深的渴望——
其供给的满足完整
即是那西方的汪洋——
名为永生——

727

Precious to Me—She still shall be—

Though She forget the name I bear—
The fashion of the Gown I wear—
The very Color of My Hair—

So like the Meadows—now—
I dared to show a Tress of Theirs
If haply—She might not despise
A Buttercup's Array—

I know the Whole—obscures the Part—
The fraction—that appeased the Heart
Till Number's Empery—
Remembered—as the Milliner's flower
When Summer's Everlasting Dower—
Confronts the dazzled Bee.

727①
对我很珍贵——她依然是——
虽然她忘记我的名字——
我衣服的款式——
我头发颜色的特质——

所以一如那些牧场——此时——
我大胆将他们一绺长发展示
假如凑巧——她不会瞧不上
一朵金凤花的盛装——

我知道整体——会模糊个体——
部分——它让心平息

---

① 题解：她不一定珍视我，几乎把我忘记，但我依然珍视她，想要对她表达，所以在牧场上摘了一朵金凤花，如一绺长发，送给她，希望她能记起我。但是对方已经有了一个整体的世界（已婚?），不会记得我这个个体，我这个能够平息她心的个体部分，压不过数字上更大的整体的作用，仅被她当成一朵女帽商佩戴的花，来忆起。这无疑令我眩晕，面对她那貌似永久的整体（婚姻），一如蜜蜂面对夏日永恒的嫁妆。

直至数字加以掌控——
被当成女帽商的花朵——怀想
当夏日永恒的嫁妆——
直面眩晕的蜜蜂。

728
Let Us play Yesterday—
I—the Girl at school—
You—and Eternity—the
Untold Tale—

Easing my famine
At my Lexicon—
Logarithm—had I—for Drink—
'Twas a dry Wine—

Somewhat different—must be—
Dreams tint the Sleep—
Cunning Reds of Morning
Make the Blind—leap—

Still at the Egg-life—
Chafing the Shell—
When you troubled the Ellipse—
And the Bird fell—

Manacles be dim—they say—
To the new Free—
Liberty—Commoner—
Never could—to me—

'Twas my last gratitude
When I slept—at night—
'Twas the first Miracle
Let in—with Light—

Can the Lark resume the Shell—
Easier—for the Sky—
Would'nt Bonds hurt more
Than Yesterday?

Would'nt Dungeons sorer frate
On the Man—free—
Just long enough to taste—
Then—doomed new—

God of the Manacle
As of the Free—
Take not my Liberty
Away from Me—

728
让我们重演昨日——
我——是在校的女孩子——
你——和永恒——是
未展开的故事——

缓解我的饥饿
在字典①里遨游——
对数——我用来——喝——
它是干葡萄酒——

有些不同——肯定——
梦给睡眠披上彩衣——
清晨诱人的红霞
令百叶窗——跳起——

---

① 字典（Lexicon）：艾米莉·狄金森在 1862 年 4 月 25 日写给文学导师希金森的信中曾说："For several years, my Lexicon – was my only companion."（L261）

仍然过着蛋一般封闭的生活——
时常把蛋壳摩挲——
当你把这椭圆打破——
鸟儿就从中掉落——

脚镣已褪色——他们说——
对于刚获释者——
自由——更常见——
对我——却不见得——

它是我最后的感激
当我歇息——在夜里——
也是最初的奇迹
出现——和光明一起——

假如云雀能重回蛋壳——
天空——更辽阔无际——
难道那羁绊不会伤害更大
胜过昨日？

难道地牢的格栅不会更冷酷
对于一个人——无拘无束——
已尝受够久——
随后——重被禁锢——

掌控镣铐以及
获释者的上帝——
别把我的自由
从我这儿夺去——

729

Alter! When the Hills do—
Falter! When the Sun

Question if His Glory
Be the Perfect One—

Surfeit! When the Daffodil
Doth of the Dew—
Even as Herself—Sir—
I will—of You—

729①
改变！当群山可以——
犹豫！当太阳
怀疑是否他的光华
完美无瑕——

贪恋！当黄水仙
对甘露确实贪得无厌——
纵使像她那样——先生——
我也会——这般对你——

730
Defrauded I a Butterfly—
The lawful Heir—for Thee—

730②
我欺骗了一只蝴蝶——
那法定的继承人——为了你——

---

① 题解：群山想改变就可以改变，太阳也可以犹豫，当它对自己的光华是否完美有怀疑，但我对你，则完全不一样！像黄水仙贪恋甘露，我始终如一，对你贪恋无厌！

② *Further Poems of Emily Dickinson* 一书的编者认为本诗是寄给一位朋友的，且随诗"随附一朵花"("Send with a flower.")。如此，诗人为了收信人（"你"）而摘了一朵花，把花的法定继承人——蝴蝶欺骗了，也就好理解了。（参见 Bianchi, Martha Dickinson, & Alfred Leete Hampson, eds. *Further Poems of Emily Dickinson*. Boston: Little, Brown and Company, 1929.）

731

"I want" —it pleaded—All its life—
I want—was chief it said
When Skill entreated it—the last—
And when so newly dead—

I could not deem it late—to hear
That single—steadfast sigh—
The lips had placed as with a "Please"
Toward Eternity—

731

"我想要"——它恳求——要它的终生——
我想要——是它反复最多的词语
当它乞求技艺①——最后一次——
当刚刚如此死去——

我不能说很迟——才听到
那一阵——长长叹息声——
那双唇仿佛携着一个"求你"
朝向永恒——

732

She rose to His Requirement—dropt
The Playthings of Her Life
To take the honorable Work
Of Woman, and of Wife—

If ought She missed in Her new Day,
Of Amplitude, or Awe—

---

① 当它乞求技艺（When Skill entreated it）：原文是倒装，正常语序应是"When it entreated Skill."。根据上下文，Skill 应喻指死神或某种超自然力量。本诗似展示了濒死之人不愿离世，因此恳求死神再给还自己的一生，但最后并未能如愿。

Or first Prospective—Or the Gold
In using, wear away,

It lay unmentioned—as the Sea
Develop Pearl, and Weed,
But only to Himself—be known
The Fathoms they abide—

732①
她应和他的要求——抛弃
她生命中各种玩具②
以承担那光荣的工作
做一个女人，一个人妻——

是否在崭新的日子里她还忆起，
那广袤，那敬畏——
或最初的憧憬——或金子
在磨砺中，渐渐消褪，

那也已无人提及——一如大海
生长着水草和珍珠，
但只有他自己——知道
它们居住的深度——

733
The Spirit is the Conscious Ear.
We actually Hear
When We inspect—that's audible—

---

① 题解：女性一旦承担了人妻的光荣工作，那么她结婚前的少女时期那些思想和想法，只有她自己知道，不会再有人提及，一如大海，只有大海自己知道自己培育的珍珠和水草身居何处。

② 玩具（Playthings）：既指玩具，也指各种玩乐嬉戏，这里或喻指女性结婚前少女时期的各种事情均如玩具或玩戏，都不太重要，只有结婚后承担作为人妻的工作是光荣的、重要的。

That is admitted—Here—

For other Services—as Sound—
There hangs a smaller Ear
Outside the Castle—that Contain—
The other—only—Hear—

733①
精神是有意识的耳朵。
当我们检视时
我们确能听见——那可听见的——
这已被承认——在这里——

至于其他事务——比如声音——
尚有一只较小的耳朵
挂在城堡外——包含这功用——
那另一只耳——仅负责——听的工作——

734
If He were living—dare I ask—
And how if He be dead—
And so around the Words I went—
Of meeting them—afraid—

I hinted Changes—Lapse of Time—
The Surfaces of Years—
I touched with Caution—lest they crack—
And show me to my fears—

Reverted to adjoining Lives—
Adroitly turning out

---

① 题解：精神（心灵）像耳朵一样，当我们内视，可以听见我们内心的声音；而在城堡（头颅）外的那另一只耳朵，只能胜任听实际声音的工作。

Wherever I suspected Graves—
'Twas prudenter—I thought—

And He—I pushed—with sudden force—
In face of the Suspense—
"Was buried" — "Buried"! "He!"
My Life just holds the Trench—

734①
他是否还活着——我胆敢问——
假如他死了是怎么个死法——
我就这样围绕这些词语兜圈——
生怕——与它们碰面——

我暗示有了变化——还有时光流逝——
我小心触及——
那些年月的表面——以免他们破裂——
展示给我使我惊惧——

转向那些毗邻的生命求助——
我巧妙地岔开一旁
当怀疑会提及坟墓——
这样谨慎一点——我想——

而对他——我推——用猛力——
直面悬念的迷蒙——
"已埋啦"——"埋啦"!"他!"
我的生命随即抱住那壕坑——

---

① 题解:时光荏苒,一切都起了变化,而"他"是死是活?"我"小心地问别人,随后又转向"他"身边的其他人求助,但当可能提到死亡时,"我"又巧妙地把话题岔开了。最后,终于狠下心,猛地推开悬念,一问究竟,得到的回答是"已埋啦",我不禁惊叫"埋啦"!"他!",顿时抱住那埋葬的壕坑。

735

Upon Concluded Lives
There's nothing cooler falls—
Than Life's sweet Calculations—
The mixing Bells and Palls—

Make Lacerating Tune—
To Ears the Dying Side—
'Tis Coronal—and Funeral—
Saluting—in the Road—

735①

对于已完结的生命
没有什么更酷的事——
胜过生命甜美的算计——
那丧钟和柩衣交织——

合成撕心的哀曲——
在逝者旁边的耳里——
那是花冠——和葬礼——
在路上——致意——

736

Have any like Myself
Investigating March,
New Houses on the Hill descried—
And possibly a Church—

That were not, We are sure—
As lately as the Snow—
And are Today—if We exist—

---

① 题解：对于死者和生者，谁更幸运？花冠和葬礼，属于谁？

Though how may this be so?

Have any like Myself
Conjectured Who may be
The Occupants of the Adobes—
So easy to the Sky—

Twould seem that God should be
The nearest Neighbor to—
And Heaven—a convenient Grace
For Show, or Company—

Have any like Myself
Preserved the Charm secure
By shunning carefully the Place
All Seasons of the Year,

Excepting March—'Tis then
My Villages be seen—
And possibly a Steeple—
Not afterward—by Men—

736①
有谁像我这样
去调查三月的景象，
发现山上有不少新房——
也许还有一座教堂——

---

① 题注：写二月的还有第1213、1320和1404首诗。对狄金森而言，三月是充满希冀的月份（"March is the Month of Expectation."P1404），她在1885年3月写给朋友海伦（Helen Hunt Jackson, 1830—1885）的一封信中也说道："Who could be ill in March, that Month of proclamation?"（L976）

我们敢肯定,那里原非如此——
直至最近下雪的季节——
今天才出现——假如我们还在——
但怎么会出现这些?

有谁像我这样
去猜谁是
这些居所的住户——
离上天近在咫尺——

看起来上帝就是
最近的邻居——
而天堂——是常见贵客
经常出现,或左右不离——

有谁像我这样
为铭记这迷人景象
一年四季
都小心避开那地方,

除了三月——正是此时
我的村庄显现——
也许还有一座教堂塔尖——
而非此后——被人看见——

737

The Moon was but a Chin of Gold
A Night or two ago—
And now she turns Her perfect Face
Upon the World below—

Her Forehead is of Amplest Blonde—
Her Cheek—a Beryl hewn—

Her Eye unto the Summer Dew
The likest I have known—

Her Lips of Amber never part—
But what must be the smile
Upon Her Friend she could confer
Were such Her Silver Will—

And what a privilege to be
But the remotest Star—
For Certainty She take Her Way
Beside Your Palace Door—

Her Bonnet is the Firmament—
The Universe—Her Shoe—
The Stars—the Trinkets at Her Belt—
Her Dimities—of Blue—

737①

月亮仅是金黄下巴一面
在此前一两夜——
如今她变成一张圆满的脸
对着下面的凡界——

她的额头泛黄——
她的颊——一抹浅蓝——
她的眼如夏日的露珠
如此相像我前所未见——

她的唇永远如琥珀——
而那笑脸

---

① 参阅与月亮有关的其他诗歌，如第429、504和629首。

一定是她献给友人的
银色祝愿——

最特别的一点
是无论星星多遥远——
她都能一路走到
你的宫门边——

她的软帽就是苍天——
宇宙——是她的鞋——
群星——是她腰带的饰件——
她的细纹服——是蓝色——

738

You said that I "was Great" —one Day—
Then "Great" it be—if that please Thee—
Or Small—or any size at all—
Nay—I'm the size suit Thee—

Tall—like the Stag—would that?
Or lower—like the Wren—
Or other hights of Other Ones
I've seen?

Tell which—it's dull to guess—
And I must be Rhinoceros
Or Mouse
At once—for Thee—

So say—if Queen it be—
Or Page—please Thee—
I'm that—or nought—
Or other thing—if other thing there be—

With just this Stipulus—
I suit Thee—

738
你说我"大"——有一天——
那就"大"吧——如果令你欢喜——
或者小——或任何尺寸——
不——我的尺寸要合你意——

高——如牡鹿——那样行么?
或低一点——像鹩鹩——
或像我见到别的动物
这么高?

请说吧——靠猜也猜不出——
我一定会变成犀牛
或老鼠
立刻——为你——

譬如说——如果皇后是你心仪——
或差役——能令你欢喜——
那我就是那个——或啥都不是——
或是别的——如果需要是别的东西——
只需有这个前提——
我得合你意——

739
I many times thought Peace had come
When Peace was far away—
As Wrecked Men—deem they sight the Land—
At Centre of the Sea—

And struggle slacker—but to prove

As hopelessly as I—
How many the fictitious Shores—
Before the Harbor be—

739

很多次我幻想和平已来到
当和平依然遥远——
一如遇船难的人——以为他们看见了陆地——
在大海中间——①

于是放松了挣扎——最后都证明
如我般无望——
还有多少虚构的海岸——
才能抵达真正的港湾——

740

You taught me Waiting with Myself—
Appointment strictly kept—
You taught me fortitude of Fate—
This—also—I have learnt—

An Altitude of Death, that could
No bitterer debar
Than Life—had done—before it—
Yet—there is a Science more—

The Heaven you know—to understand
That you be not ashamed
Of Me—in Christ's bright Audience
Upon the further Hand—

---

① 在大海中间——（At Centre of the Sea -）：狄金森在1864年9月写给嫂子苏珊的一封信（L294）就以这一句开头，而本诗写于1863年。

740①

你教我独自等候——
要严守此前的约定——
你教我对命运的坚守——
这一点——我也学会——已经——

一种死亡的高度，它的阻止
远不及
生命严厉——已完成——在此前——②
然而——其中还有更深的科学道理——

在你所知的天堂——你会理解
你决不会因我
蒙羞——在明亮的基督面前
在那更远的手上——③

741

Drama's Vitallest Expression is the Common Day
That arise and set about Us—
Other Tragedy

---

① 题解："你"教我守诺，对命运虔诚，我均已做到。死亡固然可以阻止我们的努力，但活着时，若我们不愿有所为，则活着时我们的生命可以更严厉地阻止我们的行动。一种死亡已经完成（"你"已经死亡），在"我"学会"你"教我的一切之前。这死亡的阻止力虽不及生命，但却有更深的科学道理在其中，即它（"你"的死亡）是一种有高度的死亡，它站上了主的右手边，如绵羊，蒙主的福泽。"你"在天堂，面见基督，不会因我而蒙羞，一方面因为你教导予我的行为，另一方面也因为我严格遵循了你的教导。

② 这三行或也可译为：高高在上的死亡，再严厉的阻止/也不及/生命——在死亡之前——所做的一切——

③ 在那更远的手上（Upon the further Hand）：参见英文钦定版《圣经·新约·马太福音》第 25 章第 33～34 节："And he shall set the sheep on his right hand, but the goats on the left. Then shall the King say unto them on his right hand, Come, ye blessed of my Father, inherit the kingdom prepared for you from the foundation of the world."（Matthew 25：33-34）.

Perish in the Recitation—
This—the best enact
When the Audience is scattered
And the Boxes shut—

"Hamlet" to Himself were Hamlet—
Had not Shakespeare wrote—
Though the "Romeo" left no Record
Of his Juliet,

It were infinite enacted
In the Human Heart—
Only Theatre recorded
Owner cannot shut—

741①
戏剧最生动的体现是那平常日子
它起起落落都与我们有关——
其他悲剧

在背诵中消逝——
这——才是最佳的表演
当观众散去
包厢紧闭——

"哈姆雷特"对其本人就是哈姆雷特——
假如莎士比亚没写过这一出——

---

① 题解：戏剧最生动的体现发生在平常日子里，因此日常生活才是最生动、最具活力的戏剧，这才是最佳的表演，它不需要戏院的观众，不需要戏院包厢。而戏院里的戏剧，在演员背诵完台词后也就结束了，只有戏院才需要台词记述。即使莎士比亚没写过《哈姆雷特》和《罗密欧与朱丽叶》，生活中也有哈姆雷特，也有罗密欧与朱丽叶的故事，他们在人类心中不断上演，无需戏院的台词，戏院老板也无法谢演。

纵然"罗密欧"也没留下
朱丽叶的任何记录,

但它总不断地上演
在人类心里——
只有戏院才需语言记述
店主也无法关闭——

742

Four Trees—upon a solitary Acre—
Without Design
Or Order, or Apparent Action—
Maintain—

The Sun—upon a Morning meets them—
The Wind—
No nearer Neighbor—have they—
But God—

The Acre gives them—Place—
They—Him—Attention of Passer by—
Of Shadow, or of Squirrel, haply—
Or Boy—

What Deed is Theirs unto the General Nature—
What Plan
They severally—retard—or further—
Unknown—

742

四棵树——立于一片孤零的土地——
未经设计

或安排,或明显的行为——
来维持——

太阳——在清晨遇见它们——
风——
它们没有比这更近的——邻居——
除了上帝——

土地给他们——空间——
它们——回赠他——过客的青睐——
阴影,或松鼠,偶尔——
还有男孩——

它们对大自然有何功绩——
什么计划
它们各自——延迟——或推进——
无从得知——

743

The Birds reported from the South—
A News express to Me—
A spicy Charge, My little Posts—
But I am deaf—Today—

The Flowers—appealed—a timid Throng—
I reinforced the Door—
Go blossom for the Bees—I said—
And trouble Me—no More—

The Summer Grace, for Notice strove—
Remote—Her best Array—
The Heart—to stimulate the Eye

Refused too utterly—

At length, a Mourner, like Myself,
She drew away austere—
Her frosts to ponder—then it was
I recollected Her—

She suffered Me, for I had mourned—
I offered Her no word—
My Witness—was the Crape I bore—
Her—Witness—was Her Dead—

Thenceforward—We—together dwelt—
I never questioned Her—
Our Contract
A Wiser Sympathy

743①

鸟儿们从南方——
向我报告一个消息——
一个浓情的嘱咐，我的这些小邮递员——
但我聋了——今天——

花儿们——请求——挤进来一点点——
我更把门户紧锁——
去对蜂儿们绽放吧——我说——
别再来——烦我——

---

① 题解："我"本已哀伤，对鸟儿捎来的消息、花儿们的请求，以及夏天的繁华和灿烂，均不在意，直至夏季将尽，转入秋霜时节，夏季也如"我"一样成为哀伤者，我才留意她，将她忆起。"我"戴着黑纱哀悼亡者，夏季则见证了自己的死亡，他们互相亲近、互相同情。

那夏天的荣华，竭力引人注意——
远远地——打扮得极美丽——
心——无法刺激眼睛
只因回绝得太彻底——

最终，一位哀伤者，像我自己，
面色严峻地抽身离去——
去思虑她的寒霜雪意①——此时
只有我将她忆起——

她容忍了我，因为我已深陷哀伤——
我没给过她一个字——
我见证的——是我戴的黑纱——
她——则见证——她的死——

随后——我们——住在了一起——
我从未对她质疑——
我们的协议
是一份更明智的彼此同情

744
Remorse—is Memory—awake—
Her Parties all astir—
A Presence of Departed Acts—
At window—and at Door—

Its Past—set down before the Soul
And lighted with a Match—
Perusal—to facilitate—
And help Belief to stretch—

---

① "去思虑她的寒霜雪意"或也可译为"只有她的冷若冰霜令人惦记"。

Remorse is cureless—the Disease
Not even God—can heal—
For 'tis His institution—and
The Adequate of Hell—

744

懊悔——是记忆——苏醒——
五味俱全——
逝去的一切重现眼前——
在窗户——和门边——

它的过去——在灵魂前停驻
把一根火柴燃亮——
方便——阅读——
也利于信念延长——

懊悔无药可医——这病
连上帝也不能——治愈——
因为这就是他的制度——也
等同于地狱——

745

Renunciation—is a piercing Virtue—
The letting go
A Presence—for an Expectation—
Not now—
The putting out of Eyes—
Just Sunrise—
Lest Day—
Day's Great Progenitor—
Outvie
Renunciation—is the Choosing
Against itself—
Itself to justify

Unto itself—
When larger function—
Make that appear—
Smaller—that Covered Vision—Here—

745①
弃绝——是一种令人揪心的德行——
是放开
当前——为一个憧憬——
而非为现在——
是视而不见——
对那日出——
以免白天——
白天古老的祖先——
抢在前
弃绝——这种抉择
违背了自己——
并自己证明自己
合理——
当那更大的功用——
使它显示——
那较小的——就成被遮盖的景象——在此——②

746
Never for Society

---

① 题解：弃绝就是放弃，放弃当前，为了一个对未来的憧憬或期望，比如放弃当前的日出，担心眼前光明的白天会遮蔽心中对未来憧憬的美好。这种放弃往往是违背了自己，且自己证明自己合理，自己说服自己。当对未来更大的憧憬或期望（"更大的功用"）使弃绝的行为（"它"）出现，那当前也就变成"那较小的"，即具有较小功用的存在，成为被"更大功用"遮蔽的存在，在当前、现在。

② 最后三行也可译为：当那更大的功用——/令它显示——/更小——也即那被遮盖的景象——在此——

意为：当对未来更大的憧憬或期望（"更大的功用"）令当前（"它"）显得较小，成了被"更大功用"遮蔽的存在（"被遮盖的景象"）时，放弃当前自然就显得合理了。

He shall seek in vain—
Who His own acquaintance
Cultivate—Of Men
Wiser Men may weary—
But the Man within

Never knew Satiety—
Better entertain
Than could Border Ballad—
Or Biscayan Hymn—
Neither introduction
Need You—unto Him—

746
他对友伴的找寻
决不会徒劳无功——
他要把人类——都培养成
他自己的熟人
再聪明的人都会累——
但内心的那一位

从不知疲惫——
反而其乐陶陶
胜过听边疆民谣——
或比斯开湾①圣歌调——
无需你
向他————介绍——

---

① 比斯开湾（Biscayan）：指"比斯开湾的"（Pertaining to the Bay of Biscay），也可指"比斯开省的"，即西班牙北部比斯开湾（Bay of Biscay）旁边的比斯开省 [Biscay (Vizcaya) Province]，位于西班牙北部和法国南部的巴斯克地区（Basque country）内。比斯开（Biscay）是法国一港口。比斯开湾（the Bay of Biscay）是大西洋上法国西部海岸和西班牙北部海岸之间的海湾，是相对危险的水域，以强劲湾流和暴风雨闻名，此水域发生过无数船难事故。

747

It dropped so low—in my Regard—
I heard it hit the Ground—
And go to pieces on the Stones
At bottom of my Mind—

Yet blamed the Fate that fractured①—*less*
Than I reviled② Myself,
For entertaining Plated Wares
Upon my Silver Shelf—

747

它坠得如此低——在我看来——
我听到它碰了地——
在石头上撞碎
在我心的最底——

但与其怨命运打碎——不如
把自己责骂,
竟然将镀银的器皿
摆上我银架——

748

Autumn—overlooked my Knitting—
Dyes—said He—have I—
Could disparage a Flamingo—
Show Me them—said I—

Cochineal—I chose—for deeming

---

① "fractured"一词在1960年的阅读版中改为"flung it"。
② "reviled"一词在1960年的阅读版中改为"denounced"。

It resemble Thee—
And the little Border—Dusker—
For resembling Me—

748
秋天——俯看我织衣——
我有——染料——他说——
足以蔑视一只火烈鸟——
拿给我看——我说——

我选了——胭脂红——因为觉得
它和你相像——
还有那条小边——暗一点——
像我一样——

749
All but Death, can be Adjusted—
Dynasties repaired—
Systems—settled in their Sockets—
Citadels—dissolved—

Wastes of Lives—resown with Colors
By Succeeding Springs—
Death—unto itself—Exception—
Is exempt from Change—

749
除了死亡，一切皆可调整——
朝代可以整饰——
体制——要适应底座——
城堡——终会消失——

生命的废墟——重焕光彩

在下一个春天——
唯独死亡——自己——是例外——
它从不改变——

750
Growth of Man—like Growth of Nature—
Gravitates within—
Atmosphere, and Sun endorse it—
But it stir—alone—

Each—it's difficult Ideal
Must achieve—Itself—
Through the solitary prowess
Of a Silent Life—

Effort—is the sole condition—
Patience of Itself—
Patience of opposing forces—
And intact Belief—

Looking on—is the Department
Of it's Audience—
But Transaction—is assisted
By no Countenance—

750
人的生长——像大自然的生长——
从内部接受引力——
有大气,和太阳帮忙——
但它自行——开启——

每一次——它艰难的理想
必须实现——靠自己——

凭藉宁静生活里
孤独无畏的勇气——

努力——是唯一条件——
对自己耐心一点——
对逆境耐心一点——
还有不变的信念——

旁观的——有一群
观众——
但问题的解决——决不靠
这些面孔——

751

My Worthiness is all my Doubt—
His Merit—all my fear—
Contrasting which, my quality
Do lowlier—appear—

Lest I should insufficient prove
For His beloved Need—
The Chiefest Apprehension
Upon my thronging Mind—

'Tis true—that Deity to stoop
Inherently incline—
For nothing higher than Itself
Itself can rest upon—

So I—the undivine abode
Of His Elect Content—
Conform my Soul—as twere a Church,
Unto Her Sacrament—

751

我的价值在于我全部的质疑——
他的卓越——是我所惧——
与之相比,我的资质
确实显得——较低——

为免露出
我不足以供亲爱的他所需——
我最大的忧虑
都隐藏在我纷扰的心里——

确实——神会包涵关照
历来都这样——
因为没有什么比他更高
他可以自作主张——

所以我——这凡俗的躯体
驻有他神圣的内涵——
让我的灵魂——仿佛是一所教堂,
领受她的圣餐——

752

So the Eyes accost—and sunder
In an Audience—
Stamped—occasionally—forever—
So may Countenance

Entertain—without addressing
Countenance of One
In a Neighboring Horizon—
Gone—as soon as known—

752
所以眼神相遇——就分离
在一个人群间——
有时——会被永远——铭记——
所以但愿脸

感到快意——而不必
面对谁的脸
在附近疆域——
才认识——就不见——

753
My Soul—accused me—And I quailed—
As Tongue of Diamond had reviled
All else accused me—and I smiled—
My Soul—that Morning—was My friend—

Her favor—is the best Disdain
Toward Artifice of Time—or Men—
But Her Disdain—'twere lighter bear
A finger of Enamelled Fire—

753
我的灵魂——声讨我——我感到害怕——
仿佛钻石舌头的辱骂
而来自别处的指责——我都能笑着对答——
我的灵魂——那天早上——是我的朋友——

她的宠爱——就是最好的鄙夷
对时间或人类的——诡计——
但她的鄙夷——若论忍受煎熬的轻浅
不如指尖珐琅质的火焰——

754

My Life had stood—a Loaded Gun—
In Corners—till a Day
The Owner passed—identified—
And carried Me away—

And now We roam in Sovereign Woods—
And now We hunt the Doe—
And every time I speak for Him—
The Mountains straight reply—

And do I smile, such cordial light
Upon the Valley glow—
It is as a Vesuvian face
Had let it's pleasure through—

And when at Night—Our good Day done—
I guard My Master's Head—
'Tis better than the Eider-Duck's
Deep Pillow—to have shared—

To foe of His—I'm deadly foe—
None stir the second time—
On whom I lay a Yellow Eye—
Or an emphatic Thumb—

Though I than He—may longer live
He longer must—than I—
For I have but the power to kill,
Without—the power to die—

754

我的生命立着——像一杆上膛的枪——

在角落——直到一天
主人经过——认出来——
把我带向遥远——

如今我们在巍巍丛林中漫游——
如今我们捕猎母鹿——
每次我替他发话——
群峰都径直回复——

我展露微笑,如此柔和光亮
在山谷里闪现——
好似一张维苏威火山的脸
上面快乐可见——

到了夜晚——愉快的一天结束——
我守在主人头边——
胜过共用那鸭绒的
大枕头——在头下垫——

对于他的敌人——我就是死仇——
没人能再动弹——
只要我用黄色的眼瞅他一瞅——
或拇指用力一按——

虽然我比他——或许活得久些
但他一定比我——活得更长——
因为我只有能力去消灭,
却没能力去死亡——

755

No Bobolink—reverse His Singing
When the only Tree
Ever He minded occupying

By the Farmer be—

Clove to the Root—
His Spacious Future—
Best Horizon—gone—
Whose Music be His
Only Anodyne—
Brave Bobolink—

755

没有哪一只食米鸟——停止歌唱
当唯一的那棵树
他曾想栖息其上
却被那农夫——

直砍到树根——
他广阔的未来——
锦绣前程——也就失掉——
他的音乐是他
唯一的止痛药——
坚强的食米鸟——

756

One Blessing had I than the rest
So larger to my Eyes
That I stopped gauging—satisfied—
For this enchanted size—

It was the limit of my Dream—
The focus of my Prayer—
A perfect—paralyzing Bliss—
Contented as Despair—

I knew no more of Want—or Cold—
Phantasms both become
For this new Value in the Soul—
Supremest Earthly Sum—

The Heaven below the Heaven above—
Obscured with ruddier Blue—
Life's Latitudes leant over—full—
The Judgment perished—too—

Why Bliss so scantily disburse—
Why Paradise defer—
Why Floods be served to Us—in Bowls—
I speculate no more—

756
相比于其余我获得的一个祝福
在我看来如此宏大
我停止了测量——非常满足——
对这令人着迷的尺码——

这是我梦想的终极——
我祈祷时所关注——
一种完美的——令人酥软的快意——
如绝望般满足——

我不再感到匮乏——或寒冷——
两者都变成了幻想
只因新增了这宝贝在我灵魂——
世间万物里它至高无上——

天堂底下的天堂——
辉映着天空的霞光——

生命的空间溢满——充盈——
最后的审判日——也已消亡——

为何极乐如此罕见——
天堂遥遥无期——
暴雨——总是倾盆而至——
所有这些我都不再深思——

757

The Mountains—grow unnoticed—
Their Purple figures rise
Without attempt—Exhaustion—
Assistance—or Applause—

In Their Eternal Faces
The Sun—with just delight
Looks long—and last—and golden—
For fellowship—at night—

757

群山——不知不觉地长高——
它们紫色的身影升上来
无须预谋——尽心竭力——
帮助——或喝彩——

在它们永恒的脸上
太阳——满心欢喜
久久凝望——最后——变成金黄——
它在找寻友谊——在夜里——

758

These—saw Visions—
Latch them softly—

These—held Dimples—
Smooth them slow—
This—addressed departing accents—
Quick—Sweet Mouth—to miss thee so—

This—We stroked—
Unnumbered Satin—
These—we held among our own—
Fingers of the Slim Aurora—
Not so arrogant—this Noon—

These—adjust—that ran to meet us—
Pearl—for Stocking—Pearl for Shoe—
Paradise—the only Palace
Fit for Her reception—now—

758①

这些——曾经看到的景象——
把它们轻轻闭起——
这些——曾经定格的酒窝——
慢慢使它们平息——
这张——曾说着别离话语——
伶俐——甜蜜的嘴——多么想念你——

它——我们抚摩——
这没有编号的绸缎——
这些——我们谨记心间——
这曙光女神的纤指——

---

① 题解：说话者在从头到脚整理一位死者的遗容。先给死者闭好眼睛；抚平脸上酒窝；抚摸手臂，那曾经光溜顺滑的皮肤如今像无需标记等级数字的绸缎；早上如女神的手指，到了中午已不再纤细轻曼；曾经跑来与"我们"相见的双脚也需调整；最后在鞋袜上点缀珍珠，大功告成，就等着天堂接纳死者了。

在正午——不再如此轻曼——

这些——调整一下——它们曾跑来与我们相见——
珍珠——缀上袜——珍珠缀上鞋——
天堂——唯一的宫殿
适合接纳她——现在——

759

He fought like those Who've nought to lose—
Bestowed Himself to Balls
As One who for a further Life
Had not a further Use—

Invited Death—with bold attempt—
But Death was Coy of Him
As Other Men, were Coy of Death—
To Him—to live—was Doom—

His Comrades, shifted like the Flakes
When Gusts reverse the Snow—
But He—was left alive Because
Of Greediness to die—

759

他打起仗来好似他已无可失去——
他让自己沉迷于枪林弹雨
仿佛在未来的生活里
已无他用武之地——

向死亡邀约——以大胆的尝试——
但死亡对他总感羞怯
就像其他人,也怯于见到死——

对于他——活着——就是毁灭——

他的战友——如雪片变换不停
当阵阵狂风将雪翻起——
但他——总能活命
因他急着去死——

760

Most she touched me by her muteness—
Most she won me by the way
She presented her small figure—
Plea itself—for Charity—

Were a Crumb my whole possession—
Were there famine in the land—
Were it my resource from starving—
Could I such a plea withstand—

Not upon her knee to thank me
Sank this Beggar from the Sky—
But the Crumb partook—departed—
And returned On High—

I supposed—when sudden
Such a Praise began
'Twas as Space sat singing
To herself—and men—

'Twas the Winged Beggar—
Afterward I learned
To her Benefactor
Making Gratitude

760①

她主要用她的静默将我触动——
她主要用那种方法赢得我认可
即展示她娇小的仪容——
用它——恳求施舍——

纵然一粒面包屑是我全部所有——
纵然大地颗粒无收——
纵然它是我免于饥饿的源头——
我又怎能拒绝这样的恳求——

她并未跪下对我表示感激
这乞讨者自天空下扑——
只把面包屑吃掉——就离去——
回到原来的高处——

我猜想——当突然
出现这样的赞美
这就像整个世界静坐着歌唱
对她自己——和人类——

其实是那位带翅的乞讨者——
我事后得知
对她的恩人
表示谢意

761

From Blank to Blank—
A Threadless Way
I pushed Mechanic feet—
To stop—or perish—or advance—

---

① 关于鸟儿对面包屑的感激,另参阅第 864 首。

Alike indifferent—

If end I gained
It ends beyond
Indefinite disclosed—
I shut my eyes—and groped as well
'Twas lighter—to be Blind—

761
从荒芜到荒芜——
在一条漫无头绪的路
我机械地迈着步——
停下——或消亡——或向前——
我都不在乎——

如果我走到了终点
其实离终点还很远
它遥远无限——
我闭上眼——摸索向前
什么都看不见——感觉更明亮——

762
The Whole of it came not at once—
'Twas Murder by degrees—
A Thrust—and then for Life a chance—
The Bliss to cauterize—

The Cat reprieves the Mouse
She eases from her teeth
Just long enough for Hope to tease—
Then mashes it to death—

'Tis Life's award—to die—

Contenteder if once—
Than dying half—then rallying
For consciouser Eclipse—

762

整个过程不是一下子完成——
而是一点一点杀死——
先是一刺——然后再放生——
让快意使其麻痹——

猫给耗子缓刑
它松开牙齿
只为伺机戏弄——
再猛然将它咬死——

死亡——是生命的奖赏——
一下子结束是一种幸福——
好过先死一半——再重整旗鼓
去接受更痛彻肺腑的落幕——

763

He told a homely tale
And spotted it with tears—
Upon his infant face was set
The Cicatrice of years—

All crumpled was the cheek
No other kiss had known
Than flake of snow, divided with
The Redbreast of the Barn—

If Mother—in the Grave—
Or Father—on the Sea—

Or Father in the Firmament—
Or Bretheren, had he—

If Commonwealth below,
Or Commonwealth above
Have missed a Barefoot Citizen—
I've ransomed it—alive—

763
他讲述一个平常的故事
还用泪水陪衬——
在他婴儿般的脸上
结有岁月的疤痕——

他面颊上皱纹频现
但不是斑斑吻迹
而是雪片，中间
有谷仓的知更鸟隔离——

如果他有母亲——在墓里——
或父亲——在海域——
或父亲在天上——
或他有，兄弟——

如果地上的国度，
或天上的国度
丢失了一位赤足公民——
我已将他活生生——救赎——

764
Presentiment—is that long Shadow—on the Lawn—
Indicatives that Suns go down—

The Notice to the startled Grass
That Darkness—is about to pass—

764

预感——是那长长的暗影——在草地上——
预示着太阳就要落山——

也在通知惊慌的小草
说是黑暗——就快来到——

765

You constituted Time—
I deemed Eternity
A Revelation of Yourself—
'Twas therefore Deity

The Absolute—removed
The Relative away—
That I unto Himself adjust
My slow idolatry—

765

你构建时间——
我认为是永恒
你揭示了自己——
因而就是神圣

绝对——将
相对移开——
我便对他调整
我缓慢的崇拜——

766

My Faith is larger than the Hills—
So when the Hills decay—
My Faith must take the Purple Wheel
To show the Sun the way—

'Tis first He steps upon the Vane—
And then—upon the Hill—
And then abroad the World He go
To do His Golden Will—

And if His Yellow feet should miss—
The Bird would not arise—
The Flowers would slumber on their Stems—
No Bells have Paradise—

How dare I, therefore, stint a faith
On which so vast depends—
Lest Firmament should fail for me—
The Rivet in the Bands

766

我的信仰大过群山——
所以当群山变枯——
我的信仰就要骑上紫色的轮子
给太阳带路——

他先踏上轮叶——
接着——来到山上——
随后走向广阔的世界
去实现他金色的愿望——

万一他黄色的脚有闪失——

鸟儿就不会起床——
花儿昏睡在枝上——
天堂也没有钟响——

所以，我怎敢，吝惜信仰
他如此关系重大——
以免苍天因为我——
箍圈上的铆钉出岔

767

To offer brave assistance
To Lives that stand alone—
When One has failed to stop them—
Is Human—but Divine

To lend an Ample Sinew
Unto a Nameless Man—
Whose Homely Benediction
No other—stopped to earn—

767

去鼎力相助
那些独立坚持的众生——
当无法加以劝阻——
这是人性——但神圣

则是提供巨大支撑
给一位不知名姓的人——
他朴素的感恩
没其他人——想要去挣——

768

When I hoped, I recollect

Just the place I stood—
At a Window facing West—
Roughest Air—was good—

Not a Sleet could bite me—
Not a frost could cool—
Hope it was that kept me warm—
Not Merino shawl—

When I feared—I recollect
Just the Day it was—
Worlds were lying out to Sun—
Yet how Nature froze—

Icicles upon my soul
Prickled Blue and Cool—
Bird went praising everywhere—
Only Me—was still—

And the Day that I despaired—
This—if I forget
Nature will—that it be Night
After Sun has set—
Darkness intersect her face—
And put out her eye—
Nature hesitate—before
Memory and I—

768
我忆起,当我怀着希望
我曾站立之地——
在一个向着西面的窗户旁——
再凛冽的空气——也觉依依——

没有雨雪能将我刺激——
没有风霜让我感到凉意——
是希望使我觉得温暖——
不是羊绒披巾的功绩——

我忆起——当我感到恐惧
曾经的那一天——
万物向着阳光铺展——
而大自然仍地冻天寒——

我的心灵结着冰凌
把我刺得又冷又痛——
鸟儿四处赞颂——
唯独我——无动于衷——

我感到绝望的那一天啊——
这——如果我忘记
大自然也会——那是在夜间
当太阳已歇息——
黑暗划破她的脸——
掏出她的眼——
大自然犹豫不决——在
记忆和我面前——

769

One and One—are One—
Two—be finished using—
Well enough for Schools—
But for Minor Choosing—

Life—just—or Death—
Or the Everlasting—

More—would be too vast
For the Soul's Comprising—

769
一加一——等于一——
已不再说——等于二——
虽然在学校里是正确无疑——
但仅是少数人的选择——

只需——生存——或死亡——
或永久——
多了——就过于庞大
心灵难以承受——

770
I lived on Dread—
To Those who know
The Stimulus there is
In Danger—Other impetus
Is numb—and Vitalless—

As 'twere a Spur—upon the Soul—
A Fear will urge it where
To go without the Sceptre's aid
Were Challenging Despair.

770
我靠恐慌而活——
了解的人知道
危险给人一种
刺激——其他的动力
没有生机——没有冲动——

仿佛是一种鞭策——对于灵魂——
恐惧驱促它向前闯
没有鬼怪的帮忙
会感到巨大的绝望。

771

None can experience stint
Who Bounty—have not known—
The fact of Famine—could not be
Except for Fact of Corn—

Want—is a meagre Art
Acquired by Reverse—
The Poverty that was not Wealth—
Cannot be Indigence.

771

没人能领会节省
如果不懂得——大方——
饥荒——不可能
除非已有收成——

缺乏——是贫瘠的艺术
靠它的反面才能获取——
如果贫乏不是一种富裕——
就不能叫一贫如洗。

772

The hallowing of Pain
Like hallowing of Heaven,
Obtains at a corporeal cost—
The Summit is not given

To Him who strives severe
At middle of the Hill—
But He who has achieved the Top—
All—is the price of All—

772
痛苦的神圣
像天堂的神圣,
需要肉体的付出才能获得——
顶峰并非馈赠

给在半山腰
奋力攀爬的人——
而是给已至山巅的人——
一切——都有一切的代价——

773
Deprived of other Banquet,
I entertained Myself—
At first—a scant nutrition—
An insufficient Loaf—

But grown by slender addings
To so esteemed a size
'Tis sumptuous enough for me—
And almost to suffice

A Robin's famine able—
Red Pilgrim, He and I—
A Berry from our table
Reserve—for charity—

773

没法参加别人的宴席,
我宴请我自己——
首先——些许的食物——
一块不敷用的面包——

但一点点增加
达到这么大一堆
对我已足够奢华——
也几乎可以应对

一只知更鸟饥饿的胃口——
我和他,那红色的朝圣者——
餐桌上一枚浆果
留出来——以供施舍——

774

It is a lonesome Glee—
Yet sanctifies the Mind—
With fair association—
Afar upon the Wind

A Bird to overhear
Delight without a Cause—
Arrestless as invisible—
A matter of the Skies.

774

这是一份孤寂的欢欣——
却可以荡涤心灵——
以美好的遐想——
抵达邈远的云淡风轻

一只鸟儿无意中偷听
这无由来的欢乐——
它无影又无形——
天空一般澄澈。

775

If Blame be my side—forfeit Me—
But doom me not to forfeit Thee—
To forfeit Thee? The very name
Is sentence from Belief—and House—

775

如果是我的错——请将我放弃——
但别让我沦落到要放弃你——
放弃你？这个词
是来自信仰——和家园的判决——

776

Purple—
The Color of a Queen, is this—
The Color of A Sun
At setting—this and Amber—
Beryl—and this, at Noon—

And when at night—Auroran widths
Fling suddenly on men—
'Tis this—and Witchcraft—nature keeps
A Rank—for Iodine—

776①

紫——
一位女士的颜色，正是这——

---

① 这是狄金森提供诗歌标题的少数几首诗之一。

一个太阳的颜色
在日落时——是紫和琥珀黄——
在正午——是浅蓝——和紫色

而在夜里——极光的辽阔
猛然铺洒在人身上——
正是紫色——以及魔力——大自然用来
为碘色——留下一行——

777

The Loneliness One dare not sound—
And would as soon surmise
As in it's Grave go plumbing
To ascertain the size—

The Loneliness whose worst alarm
Is lest itself should see—
And perish from before itself
For just a scrutiny—

The Horror not to be surveyed—
But skirted in the Dark—
With Consciousness suspended—
And Being under Lock—

I fear me this—is Loneliness—
The Maker of the soul
It's Caverns and it's Corridors
Illuminate—or seal—

777

人不敢探测孤独——
但随即就去揣摩
仿佛勘察它的坟墓
以确定其规模——

孤独最严厉的警告
是别让它看见——
以免枯萎在它面前
只因细看了一眼——

恐怖的事别去揭开——
就让它缭绕在黑暗里——
不要醒来——
一直被锁闭——

我以此让自己恐惧——这孤独——
这灵魂的缔造者
它的走廊和洞窟
要么发光——要么封固——

778

This that would greet—an hour ago—
Is quaintest Distance—now—
Had it a Guest from Paradise—
Nor glow, would it, nor bow—

Had it a notice from the Noon
Nor beam would it nor warm—
Match me the Silver Reticence—
Match me the Solid Calm—

778①
这还会打招呼的一位——在一个小时前——
如今——已距离杳远——
假如有一位宾客来自天堂——
它,既不躬身行礼,也不会热情满面——

假如有一则正午发出的消息
它既不会露笑靥也不感温馨——
让我也似这般银白的无语——
让我也似这般真切的安宁——

779
The Service without Hope—
Is tenderest, I think—
Because 'tis unsustained
By stint—Rewarded Work—

Has impetus of Gain—
And impetus of Goal—
There is no Diligence like that
That knows not an Until—

779
毫无希望的劳作——
我认为,最脆弱——
因为它没有定额
支撑——有回报的工作——

有利益推动——

---

① 题解:这一小时前还能打招呼的一位,如今已死去,成为死尸一具。纵有天堂来客,它也无法起身热情行礼迎接;纵有任何好消息传来,它无法再露出笑容,感觉不到温暖。"我"看到这一切,只愿自己也如眼前景象一般静默和安宁。

有目标刺激——
不会有所谓勤奋努力
若不知何时截止——

780

The Truth—is stirless—
Other force—may be presumed to move—
This—then—is best for confidence—
When oldest Cedars swerve—

And Oaks untwist their fists—
And Mountains—feeble—lean—
How excellent a Body, that
Stands without a Bone—

How vigorous a Force
That holds without a Prop—
Truth stays Herself—and every man
That trusts Her—boldly up—

780

真理——静止——
其他力——可以假定会位移——
这一点——这么说——最令人有信心——
当最古老的雪松突然弯曲——

而橡树松开拳头——
群山——无力地——斜倚——
多棒的躯体,如果
无需骨头也能站立——

多么强大的力
不需支撑也能保持——

真理她兀自不动——每个人
凡相信她的——都坚定挺直——

781

To wait an Hour—is long—
If Love be just beyond—
To wait Eternity—is short—
If Love reward the end—

781

等待一小时——太长——
如果爱就在近旁——
等待永远——也短暂——
如果最终有爱补偿——

782

There is an arid Pleasure—
As different from Joy—
As Frost is different from Dew—
Like element—are they—

Yet one—rejoices Flowers—
And one—the Flowers abhor—
The finest Honey—curdled—
Is worthless—to the Bee—

782

有一种枯燥的愉悦——
不同于欢乐——
就如霜不同于露——
虽然成分相似——两者——

但一个——让花儿开怀——

另一个——被花儿憎恨——
再好的蜜————旦腐坏——
对于蜜蜂——也无价值——

783
The Birds begun at Four o'clock—
Their period for Dawn—
A Music numerous as space—
But neighboring as Noon—

I could not count their Force—
Their Voices did expend
As Brook by Brook bestows itself
To multiply the Pond.

Their Witnesses were not—
Except occasional man—
In homely industry arrayed—
To overtake the Morn—

Nor was it for applause—
That I could ascertain—
But independent Ecstasy
Of Deity and Men—

By Six, the Flood had done—
No Tumult there had been
Of Dressing, or Departure—
And yet the Band was gone—

The Sun engrossed the East—
The Day controlled the World—
The Miracle that introduced
Forgotten, as fulfilled.

783
众鸟在四点开始——
它们黎明的功课——
一种音乐宏大似太空——
但邻近如正午在侧——

我无法描绘它们的威力——
它们的歌声源源不断
像一条条小溪献出自己
让池塘水涨。

你看不到它们——
除了偶尔有人——
在日常的忙碌里特意安排——
赶上这早晨——

它也不求赞誉——
这一点我能确定——
而是兀自的狂喜
源自人类和神灵——

到六点，歌声的流淌止息——
没有一丁点骚动
在妆扮，或离开的过程——
但乐队已无影踪——

东方在阳光里沉迷——
白昼控制了世界——
曾经出现的奇迹
被遗忘，仿佛已圆满收场。

784

Bereaved of all, I went abroad—
No less bereaved was I
Upon a New Peninsula—
The Grave preceded me—

Obtained my Lodgings, ere myself—
And when I sought my Bed—
The Grave it was reposed upon
The Pillow for my Head—

I waked to find it first awake—
I rose—It followed me—
I tried to drop it in the Crowd—
To lose it in the Sea—

In Cups of artificial Drowse
To steep it's shape away—
The Grave—was finished—but the Spade
Remained in Memory—

784

丧失一切之后，我出走国外——
我丧失的并未见少
在一个新半岛——
那坟墓比我先到——

抢占了我住所，在我之前——
当我找我的床——
却见坟墓正安息
在我枕头上——

我睡醒，发现它已先醒——

我起身——它跟我起来——
我试图将它抛弃在人群——
遗落在大海——

浸泡在一杯杯的假寐里
让它的形状消弭——
坟墓——消失了——但那铁铲的形象
仍留在记忆里——

785

They have a little Odor—that to me
Is metre—nay—'tis melody—
And spiciest at fading—indicate—
A Habit—of a Laureate—

785

他们发出些微的香气——在我心里
是韵律——不——是乐曲——
凋谢时最是芬芳馥郁——暗示——
一位桂冠诗人的——惯例——

786

Severer Service of myself
I—hastened to demand
To fill the awful Vacuum
Your life had left behind—

I worried Nature with my Wheels
When Her's had ceased to run—
When she had put away Her Work
My own had just begun.

I strove to weary Brain and Bone—

To harass to fatigue
The glittering Retinue of nerves—
Vitality to clog

To some dull comfort Those obtain
Who put a Head away
They knew the Hair to—
And forget the color of the Day—

Affliction would not be appeased—
The Darkness braced as firm
As all my strategem had been
The Midnight to confirm—

No Drug for Consciousness—can be—
Alternative to die
Is Nature's only Pharmacy
For Being's Malady—

786①
我自己更严苛的工作
是我——急忙要求填充
你的生命留下的
可怕真空——

我的轮子让大自然忧虑

---

① 题解：有人死去，"我"哀痛不已，只有更严苛的工作，以填补对方离去留下的可怕的精神真空。自然遵循昼行夜息的规律，而我却昼夜不停地运转，令自然都担忧。我昼夜清醒，目的是让自己身心疲惫，使自己的神经也精竭力衰，以像一些获得了麻木的慰藉的人一样，可以麻木不仁，可以忘记曾经相熟的头颅，可以忘记曾经精彩的日子。这种昼夜不息的苦痛不会缓解，精神的黑暗仍会坚持，一如我仍会坚持努力解除黑暗的各种策略，午夜可以证实我一直不眠不休。这种对哀痛的沉溺没有任何药物可以唤醒，除非死亡。

当她轮子的转动已停止——
当她已将她的工作放弃
我的才刚开始。

我努力使身心疲惫——
折磨至精竭力衰
针对神经那群闪烁的随从——
将其活力阻碍

对那些得到麻木慰藉者
他们已把一颗头颅抛开
虽然熟知其毛发所在——
也忘了白日的色彩——

苦恼不会纾解——
黑暗仍坚持不懈
一如我所用的所有策略
午夜可证实这一切——

没有任何唤醒的药物——能够——
将死亡代替
这是大自然的唯一药方
专治生命的病疾——

787

Such is the Force of Happiness—
The Least—can lift a Ton
Assisted by it's stimulus—

Who Misery—sustain—
No Sinew can afford—
The Cargo of Themselves—

Too infinite for Consciousness'
Slow capabilities.

787
这就是快乐的威力——
最少的一点——能将一吨举起
只要得到激励——

它能把苦难——承受——
没有哪块筋肉能够——
它们自身的货物无限——
超出了意识
迟缓的能力。

788
Joy to have merited the Pain—
To merit the Release—
Joy to have perished every step—
To Compass Paradise—

Pardon—to look upon thy face—
With these old fashioned Eyes—
Better than new—could be—for that—
Though bought in Paradise—

Because they looked on thee before—
And thou hast looked on them—
Prove Me—My Hazel Witnesses
The features are the same—

So fleet thou wert, when present—
So infinite—when gone—
An Orient's Apparition—

Remanded of the Morn—

The Height I recollect—
'Twas even with the Hills—
The Depth upon my Soul was notched—
As Floods—on Whites of Wheels—

To Haunt—till Time have dropped
His last Decade away,
And Haunting actualize—to last
At least—Eternity—

788
很高兴领受了痛苦——
以获得释放——
很高兴毁灭在每一步——
以拥抱天堂——

请原谅——看你的脸——
用这双老式的眼——
胜过用新的——来做——这事——
虽是在天堂购置——

因他们从前看过你——
你对他们也曾眼见——
请向我证实——我淡褐色的见证人
说那些特征没什么改变——

你的出现，多么短促——
你的消失——多么无限——
好似一个东方的魅影——
将黎明遣返——

我能想起的高度——
甚至堪比群山——
而在我灵魂中的深度——
如洪水的印记——铭刻于轮子上的白点——

魂牵梦萦——直至时光
将他最后十年抛丢，
而魂梦终成真——持续
至少——到不朽——

789

On a Columnar Self—
How ample to rely
In Tumult—or Extremity—
How good the Certainty

That Lever cannot pry—
And Wedge cannot divide
Conviction—That Granitic Base—
Though None be on our Side—

Suffice Us—for a Crowd—
Ourself—and Rectitude—
And that Assembly—not far off
From furthest Spirit—God—

789

倚靠圆柱般的自己——
多么宽敞
在喧嚣——或绝境里——
那稳定的感觉多舒坦

杠杆不能撼动——

楔子无法撬开
确信——那是花岗岩的底座——
虽然我们身边没一个人存在——

我们足以——抵得上一群人——
凭我们自己——和正气——
而那个群体——也不远
离那最遥远的神灵——上帝——

790

Nature—the Gentlest Mother is,
Impatient of no Child—
The feeblest—or the waywardest—
Her Admonition mild—

In Forest—and the Hill—
By Traveller—be heard—
Restraining Rampant Squirrel—
Or too impetuous Bird—

How fair Her Conversation—
A Summer Afternoon—
Her Household—Her Assembly—
And when the Sun go down—

Her Voice among the Aisles
Incite the timid prayer
Of the minutest Cricket—
The most unworthy Flower—

When all the Children sleep—
She turns as long away
As will suffice to light Her lamps—

Then bending from the Sky—

With infinite Affection—
And infiniter Care—
Her Golden finger on Her lip—
Wills Silence—Everywhere—

790
大自然——是最温柔的母亲,
对孩子总是循循善诱——
无论是最弱小的——还是最任性的——
她的教导都那么温柔——

在森林——和山岗——
过路者——都能听到——
她约束狂妄的松鼠——
或过于急躁的小鸟——

她的话语多么动听——
在一个夏日的午后——
在她的宅屋——对她的家族——
而当日落山头——

她的声音在林间小道
将低低的祈祷激发
自那最细小的蟋蟀——
催开最微不足道的花——

等全部孩子入眠——
她才转身远离
远到足以点亮她的灯盏——
然后从天空俯身下去——

怀着无限的爱意——
和更无限的关怀——
她金色的手指放在唇际——
示意万物宁谧——无所不在——

791

God gave a Loaf to every Bird—
But just a Crumb—to Me—
I dare not eat it—tho' I starve—
My poignant luxury—

To own it—touch it—
Prove the feat—that made the Pellet mine—
Too happy—for my Sparrow's chance—
For Ampler Coveting—

It might be Famine—all around—
I could not miss an Ear—
Such Plenty smiles upon my Board—
My Garner shows so fair—

I wonder how the Rich—may feel—
An Indiaman—An Earl—
I deem that I—with but a Crumb—
Am Sovreign of them all—

791

上帝给每只鸟一块面包——
但只给我——一粒——
我不敢吃——虽然我正受饥饿煎熬——
这辛酸的奢侈待遇——

拥有它——触到它——
证明了我的功绩——即那一粒已属于我——
太高兴了——我的麻雀有机会——
贪求更多——

到处——或正闹饥荒——
我不会去想念一棵麦穗的身影——
这么富足的膳食令我笑容绽放——
我的谷仓显得如此丰盈——

我不知富人——怎么想——
譬如一位伯爵———一位跑印度的船商——
我认为我——虽只有一粒面包屑——
却比他们更高高在上——

792

Through the strait pass of suffering—
The Martyrs—even—trod.
Their feet—upon Temptations—
Their faces—upon God—

A stately—shriven—Company—
Convulsion—playing round—
Harmless—as streaks of Meteor—
Upon a Planet's Bond—

Their faith—the everlasting troth—
Their Expectation—fair—
The Needle—to the North Degree—
Wades—so—thro' polar Air!

792①

穿过苦难的狭窄通道——
那群殉道士——行进——整齐划一。
脚踩——诱惑——
面朝——上帝——

庄重——忏悔的———群——
哄笑——在四周游弋——
并无伤害——像流星划过——
环绕地球的大气——

他们的信念——永恒的誓言——
他们的憧憬——无比美丽——
指针——指向北面——
所以——跋涉——穿越极地的空气!

793

Grief is a Mouse—
And chooses Wainscot in the Breast
For His Shy House—
And baffles quest—

Grief is a Thief—quick startled—
Pricks His Ear—report to hear
Of that Vast Dark—
That swept His Being—back—

Grief is a Juggler—boldest at the Play—

---

① 本诗是艾米莉·狄金森1862年初（富兰克林版认为是1861年6月）写给朋友鲍尔斯的一封信的结尾，此前的内容是："If you doubted my Snow – for a moment – you never will – again – I know – Because I could not say it – I fixed it in the Verse – for you to read – when your thought wavers, for such a foot as mine – " （L251）

Lest if He flinch—the eye that way
Pounce on His Bruises—One—say—or Three—
Grief is a Gourmand—spare His luxury—

Best Grief is Tongueless—before He'll tell—
Burn Him in the Public Square—
His Ashes—will
Possibly—if they refuse—How then know—
Since a Rack could'nt coax a syllable—now

793
悲伤是一只老鼠——
选择胸中一块板壁
做他不起眼的住处——
以迷惑追击——

悲伤是一个贼——易受惊吓——
他竖起耳朵——听人提起
那巨大黑暗——
就能将他的魂——勾回去——

悲伤是一个杂耍者——表演最卖力——
唯恐他一畏缩——盯着看的眼
会揪住他痛处——比如说——一处——或三处——
悲伤是一个嗜食者——请恕他贪吃无厌——

真正的悲伤无言——除非他自己宣扬——
将他焚烧在广场——
他的灰烬——会讲
也许——但如果灰烬不说——那谁能知——
既然拷问架也诱不出一句话——此时

794

A Drop Fell on the Apple Tree—
Another—on the Roof—
A Half a Dozen kissed the Eaves—
And made the Gables laugh—

A few went out to help the Brook
That went to help the Sea—
Myself Conjectured were they Pearls—
What Necklace could be—

The Dust replaced, in Hoisted Roads—
The Birds jocoser sung—
The Sunshine threw his Hat away—
The Bushes—spangles flung—

The Breezes brought dejected Lutes—
And bathed them in the Glee—
Then Orient showed a single Flag,
And signed the Fete away—

794

一滴落在苹果树上——
另一滴——落在屋顶——
好几滴亲吻房檐——
惹得山墙笑不停——

有一些在外面帮小溪
小溪去帮海洋——
我径自猜如果他们是珍珠——
做成项链会咋样——

尘埃回到原处，在隆起的路上——

鸟儿唱得更欢——
太阳甩掉帽子——
丛林——晶光闪闪——

微风飘来郁郁的琴音——
让它们沉浸在欢乐里——
东方随后涌现一面旗,
把喜庆一扫而去——

795

Her final Summer was it—
And yet We guessed it not—
If tenderer industriousness
Pervaded Her, We thought

A further force of life
Developed from within—
When Death lit all the shortness up
It made the hurry plain—

We wondered at our blindness
When nothing was to see
But Her Carrara Guide post—
At Our Stupidity—

When duller than our dullness
The Busy Darling lay—
So busy was she—finishing—
So leisurely—were We—

795①

这是她最后一个夏季——
但我们猜不是这样——
如果她还浑身洋溢
更殷勤的忙碌,我们想

生命更深的力量
从内部涌现——
当死亡把全部短缺点亮
那种匆匆显而易见——

我们纳闷什么也看不见
当眼前空无一物
唯有她的大理石②路标——
指向我们的糊涂——

比我们的迟钝还迟钝
那亲爱的大忙人躺低——
她曾多么忙碌——此时都已结束——
而我们——曾多么安逸——

796

Who Giants know, with lesser Men
Are incomplete, and shy—

---

① 题解:一个人准备要离世了,这是她最后一个夏季,但周围的人不知道,也不信,因为看到她比以前更殷勤、更忙碌,不像将要离世的样子。"我们"纳闷为何眼前没有什么明显迹象,"我们"竟然就什么也没看见,什么也没看出来。最后,当她离世了,"我们"就只看到了墓碑,而这墓碑,就像一块指路的路标,指向我们曾经的糊涂。我们那位亲爱的大忙人躺下死去了,如今"她"比我们曾经的迟钝还要迟钝,她曾经的忙碌也结束了,而我们一直很安逸,无所事事。

② 大理石(Carrara):也可直译为"卡拉拉",指意大利中西部托斯卡纳区(Tuscany)一个镇,自古罗马时期起即以其出产的白色大理石闻名。它是欧洲最负盛名的石材产区,这里出产的卡拉拉石材在世界各地广泛使用。

For Greatness, that is ill at ease
In minor Company—

A Smaller, could not be perturbed—
The Summer Gnat displays—
Unconscious that his single Fleet
Do not comprise the skies—

796①
所谓巨人,人类罕见
既颇害羞,也不全面——
因为伟大,总局促不安
当与渺小为伴——

那较小的,没有烦扰——
夏天出现的蚊虫——
不会想到他单独一支舰队
构不成天空——

797

By my Window have I for Scenery
Just a Sea—with a Stem—
If the Bird and the Farmer—deem it a "Pine" —
The Opinion will serve—for them—

It has no Port, nor a "Line" —but the Jays—
That split their route to the Sky—
Or a Squirrel, whose giddy Peninsula

---

① 题解:人们所知的巨人,在人类中少之又少(lesser Men),一般会让人觉得有些害羞和不够全面(即有所欠缺),原因在于把巨人的伟大(Greatness)和常人的渺小(minor)放在一起为伴,总不免令巨人局促不安。而那些较小的就没有这种困扰,比如小小的蚊蚋,可以尽情显示自己,意识不到即使一支蚊蚋舰队飞驶过天空,也不可能遮蔽原来的天空,构成一个新天空,当然,它也不会去想这些。

May be easier reached—this way—

For Inlands—the Earth is the under side—
And the upper side—is the Sun—
And it's Commerce—if Commerce it have—
Of Spice—I infer from the Odors borne—

Of it's Voice—to affirm—when the Wind is within—
Can the Dumb—define the Divine?
The Definition of Melody—is—
That Definition is none—

It—suggests to our Faith—
They—suggest to our Sight—
When the latter—is put away
I shall meet with Conviction I somewhere met
That Immortality—

Was the Pine at my Window a "Fellow
Of the Royal" Infinity?
Apprehensions—are God's introductions—
To be hallowed—accordingly—

797①

在我窗边的风景
只有一片海——带一根茎枝——
如果鸟儿和农夫——把它看作一棵"松树"——

---

① 题解：我窗户边有一棵茂密的松树，由一根树干撑起，上面有樫鸟和松鼠，它们自松树飞向天空。松树像一片内陆，下面是地球，上面是太阳，松树的贸易是香料，因它芳香馥郁。当风吹动松树内部发出声音，那旋律是天籁之音，难以定义，非人类可以解析。那旋律启示了我们对天堂的信念，那旋律和松树一起启示了我们的眼界，假如把旋律和松树抛开一边，进入冥想，"我"便会在冥想中遇见曾经遇见过的永恒。所以窗户边的那颗松树不是普通的松树，她恐怕是无限学会的会员。恐惧，往往是遇见上帝的前兆，那棵松树引人恐惧，据此，它被视为神圣，是很自然的事。

这个看法对他们——也合适——

没有港口，也没有"航线"——只有樫鸟——
岔开飞向天空的旅途——
或一只松鼠，它那令人目眩的半岛
或许更易抵达——走这条线路——

说到内陆——地球在下边——
上面——是太阳——
它的贸易——假如有贸易——
就是香料——我的推断源自那馨香——

要确定——它的声音——当风从内部刮起——
难道哑巴——能将神圣解析？
旋律的定义——就是——
没有定义——

它——启示我们的信念——
它们——启示我们的眼——
当后者——被放置一边
我定会遇见我曾在某处邂逅过的
那位永生——

我窗边的松树是否
"英国皇家"无限学会的会员①？
恐惧——是引见上帝的门槛——
被捧为神圣——很自然——

798

She staked her Feathers—Gained an Arc—
Debated—Rose again—

---

① 原文"Fellow Of the Royal"的全称应是"Fellow of the Royal Society"（英国皇家学会会员）。

This time—beyond the estimate
Of Envy, or of Men—

And now, among Circumference—
Her steady Boat be seen—
At home—among the Billows—As
The Bough where she was born—

798①
她用她的羽毛做赌注——赢得了一个弧——
争论之后——再次升起——
这一次——超乎
妒忌，或人们的估计——

如今，四周万物里——
可见她平稳的船只——
自如地——随波——仿佛
她生于其中的树枝——

799
Despair's advantage is achieved
By suffering—Despair—
To be assisted of Reverse
One must Reverse have bore—

The Worthiness of Suffering like
The Worthiness of Death
Is ascertained by tasting—

As can no other Mouth

---

① 题解：本诗或描述雏鸟试飞的情景。

Of Savors—make us conscious—
As did ourselves partake—
Affliction feels impalpable
Until Ourselves are struck—

799
绝望的好处可以获得
通过忍受——绝望——
要受益于逆境
必需亲历逆境——

受苦的价值
就像死亡的价值
需要品尝才确知——

正如没有任何人的嘴

去品味——能让我们感知——
胜过我们亲自尝试——
苦难靠感觉无法触及
直至我们受到打击——

800
Two—were immortal twice—
The privilege of few—
Eternity—obtained—in Time—
Reversed Divinity—

That our ignoble Eyes
The quality conceive
Of Paradise superlative—
Through their Comparative.

800①

二——是两次不朽——
这是少数人的特权——
永恒——依靠时间——获取——
就将神圣逆转——

是我们卑微的眼
构想出
天堂的最高级——
通过对比。

801

I play at Riches—to appease
The Clamoring for Gold—
It kept me from a Thief, I think,
For often, overbold

With Want, and Opportunity—
I could have done a Sin
And been Myself that easy Thing
An independent Man—

But often as my lot displays
Too hungry to be borne
I deem Myself what I would be—
And novel Comforting

My Poverty and I derive—

---

① 题解：生前和死后都是不朽，只有少数人才有这两次不朽。生前依靠时间获得永恒的做法，逆转了神圣的原意，其实，是凡人用低下的肉眼，在想象中比较生前和死后，主观地把天堂的品级（quality）构想为最高级而已。换言之，只有少数人认识到今生和来生同等重要，而大多数人则认为来生更重要，但其实那只是他们的主观设想而已。

We question if the Man—
Who own—Esteem the Opulence—
As We—Who never Can—

Should ever these exploring Hands
Chance Sovereign on a Mine—
Or in the long—uneven term
To win, become their turn—

How fitter they will be—for Want—
Enlightening so well—
I know not which, Desire, or Grant—
Be wholly beautiful—

801
我戏谑财富——以平息
对金子的叫嚷——
这让我避免成贼,我认为,
因为时常,过于鲁莽

由于贫乏,以及机遇——
我可能会犯下罪
让自己轻易得到那东西
成为一个自立的人——

但时常如我的命运所示
因太饥渴而难以排解
我就把自己看成我想要的样子——
以得到奇异的慰藉

慰藉我的贫穷和我自己——
我们怀疑那人——
那拥有者——是否会尊重财富——

一如我们——这些从未富有的人——

万一哪天这些追求的手
碰巧拥有一座矿山——
或长久——坎坷的一段时间后
终于成功，轮到他们如愿——

他们会更适宜——因为贫乏——
带来了如此大的启迪——
我不知是哪一个，是渴望进取，还是赐予——
令人惬意无比——

802

Time feels so vast that were it not
For an Eternity—
I fear me this Circumference
Engross my Finity—

To His exclusion, who prepare
By Processes of Size
For the Stupendous Vision
Of his diameters—

802

时间给人感觉如此宽广
假如它不是奔向永恒——
我担心这种浩瀚
会耗尽我有限的一生——

排除他，他忙着
通过规模的进程
准备那巨大图景
为他的直径——

803

Who Court obtain within Himself
Sees every Man a King—
And Poverty of Monarchy
Is an interior thing—

No Man depose
Whom Fate Ordain—
And Who can add a Crown
To Him who doth continual
Conspire against His Own

803

在内心获得朝廷的人
把每个人看作王——
因而君王的贫乏
是一件内部事项——

没人能推翻
命定的东西——
而谁又能让
不断密谋的人
戴上皇冠

804

No Notice gave She, but a Change—
No Message, but a Sigh—
For Whom, the Time did not suffice
That She should specify.

She was not warm, though Summer shone
Nor scrupulous of cold
Though Rime by Rime, the steady Frost

Upon Her Bosom piled—

Of shrinking ways—she did not fright
Though all the Village looked—
But held Her gravity aloft—
And met the gaze—direct—

And when adjusted like a Seed
In careful fitted Ground
Unto the Everlasting Spring
And hindered but a Mound

Her Warm return, if so she chose—
And We—imploring drew—
Removed our invitation by
As Some She never knew—

804
她没给通知,只有一个变化——
也没有口信,只有一声叹气——
对这一切,时间不够充裕
能让她一一辨析。

她并不觉温暖,虽然夏日光芒闪闪
也感觉不到一丝寒凉
虽然一层层,愈积愈厚的白霜
堆上她胸膛——

她并不害怕——畏手畏足
虽然全村人都对她注目——
而是高昂她的威仪——
直面——注视——

当像一粒种子
在精心挑选的地里
适应了永久的春季
只有坟墓阻止

她温暖的回归,假如她这样决定——
任我们——恳求一遍遍——
仍移除我们的邀请
仿佛她从未谋面——

805

This Bauble was preferred of Bees—
By Butterflies admired
At Heavenly—Hopeless Distances—
Was justified of Bird—

Did Noon—enamel—in Herself
Was Summer to a Score
Who only knew of Universe—
It had created Her.

805

这小玩意深为蜜蜂所喜——
蝴蝶也心仪
在天堂般的——无望的远地——
鸟儿也证实合理——

假如正午——给她——涂釉
她就是夏季对于地球生物①
他们只知宇宙——
是宇宙将她造出。

---

① 地球生物(Score):据 *Emily Dickinson Lexicon*,Score 有 group、number of earthly beings 之意。

806

A Plated Life—diversified
With Gold and Silver Pain
To prove the presence of the Ore
In Particles—'tis when

A Value struggle—it exist—
A Power—will proclaim
Although Annihilation pile
Whole Chaoses on Him—

806

镀过的生命——各异
有金也有银的苦恼
证明矿石显示自己
以微粒——只要

一种价值争取——它就存在——
就有一种力量——宣示
纵然毁灭会把整个混乱
往他身上堆集——

807

Expectation—is Contentment—
Gain—Satiety—
But Satiety—Conviction
Of Nescessity

Of an Austere trait in Pleasure—
Good, without alarm
Is a too established Fortune—
Danger—deepens Sum—

807
期待——是幸福——
得到——是餍足——
而餍足——就表明
理应

快乐含有简朴特性——
一味舒服，缺乏警醒
是一笔太过稳当的财富——
有危险——才能加深其总数——

808①
So set it's Sun in Thee
What Day be dark to me
What Distance far
So I the Ships may see
That touch—how seldomly
Thy Shore?

808
只要它的太阳落在你心里
对我而言还有什么日子黑漆漆
还有什么距离遥远
只要我看见那些船只
停靠——好不容易
你的海岸？

809
Unable are the Loved to die
For Love is Immortality,

---

① 1960年阅读版在第二、三、五行末加了破折号。第三行"far"前也加了破折号。

Nay, it is Deity—

Unable they that love—to die
For Love reforms Vitality
Into Divinity.

809
被爱者不会死去
因为爱永生，
不，它神圣——

爱人者不会——死去
因为爱让生命
具有神性。

810
Her Grace is all she has—
And that, so least displays—
One Art to recognize, must be,
Another Art, to praise.

810
上天的恩典是她全部所有——
而且，难得显示一回——
要识别一种技艺，必须，
对另一种技艺，赞美。

811
The Veins of other Flowers
The Scarlet Flowers are
Till Nature leisure has for Terms
As "Branch," and "Jugular."

We pass, and she abides.
We conjugate Her Skill
While She creates and federates
Without a syllable.

811

其他花的脉茎
都叫腥红花这个词
直到大自然有空起名
如"颈脉",和"分枝"。

我们会逝去,而她留驻。
我们化用她的方法
而她只创造和联合
一言不发。

812

A Light exists in Spring
Not present on the Year
At any other period—
When March is scarcely here

A Color stands abroad
On Solitary Fields
That Science cannot overtake
But Human Nature feels.

It waits upon the Lawn,
It shows the furthest Tree
Upon the furthest Slope you know
It almost speaks to you.

Then as Horizons step
Or Noons report away
Without the Formula of sound
It passes and we stay—

A quality of loss
Affecting our Content
As Trade had suddenly encroached
Upon a Sacrament.

812
一种光明存在于春天
而不出现在
一年中的其他时间——
当三月刚刚到来

一种色彩站立在外
在寂寥的田野
科学尚不明白
但人性已能感觉。

它静待在草地，
映出那最远的树
在那最远的山坡你知道
它几乎要和你攀谈。

随后当地平线走开去
或正午说要别离
没有一点正式声息
它就消失而我们还在原地——

一种失落的特质
影响我们心绪
就像交易突然侵入
一场圣礼。

813

This quiet Dust was Gentleman and Ladies
And Lads and Girls—
Was laughter and ability and Sighing
And Frocks and Curls.

This Passive Place a Summer's nimble mansion
Where Bloom and Bees
Exists an Oriental Circuit
Then cease, like these—

813

这宁静的尘是先生和女士
以及少男少女——
是欢笑、才干和叹息
还有卷发和长衣。

这静穆之地是夏日一座轻灵的宅第
那里花朵和蜜蜂
笑语盈盈围坐一起①
然后停止不动，像这些——

814

One Day is there of the Series
Termed Thanksgiving Day.

---

① 笑语盈盈围坐一起（Exists an Oriental Circuit）："Oriental" 取 *Emily Dickinson Lexicon* 提供的寓意：living、alive、active、lively。

Celebrated part at Table
Part in Memory.

Neither Patriarch nor Pussy
I dissect the Play
Seems it to my Hooded thinking
Reflex Holiday.

Had there been no sharp Subtraction
From the early Sum—
Not an Acre or a Caption
Where was once a Room—

Not a Mention, whose small Pebble
Wrinkled any Sea,
Unto Such, were such Assembly
Twere Thanksgiving Day.

814①

一系列日子中有一个
叫感恩节。
部分在餐桌上庆祝
部分在记忆里关切。

既无家长也无猫咪
我把游戏分解
仿佛它对于我沉重的思绪
就意味着佳节。

---

① 题解：庆祝感恩节，在餐桌旁吃完饭，就剩下回忆。家中既无他人也无宠物，只能我一个人随意过这个感恩节，仿佛随意玩一个游戏。对于我这个有沉重思绪的人，这就算过节了。假如（家中人的）总数没有锐减，在那曾经的房间（饭厅）里，就不会贴有标示名字的标题，也不会有空无人坐的椅子（那一英亩），也不会提到某人曾用小卵石可以激起海面的涟漪。假如真有这么多人汇聚一起，那才叫过节。

假如没把原先的总数
大幅削减——
就没有说明的标题或那一英亩
在那曾经的房间——

也没人提及,其小小卵石
可以激起任何海面的涟漪,
这些,如果真有这样的汇聚
那才叫感恩节佳期。

815

The Luxury to apprehend
The Luxury 'twould be
To look at Thee a single time
An Epicure of Me

In whatsoever Presence makes
Till for a further Food
I scarcely recollect to starve
So first am I supplied—

The Luxury to meditate
The Luxury it was
To banquet on thy Countenance
A Sumptuousness bestows

On plainer Days, whose Table far
As Certainty can see
Is laden with a single Crumb
The Consciousness of Thee.

815

若说领略什么算奢侈
那奢侈就是

只看你一次
我便如美食家一样贪食

不论你以什么形象出现
直至下一次美食
我几乎想不起有过饿感
这是我第一次获得如此待遇——

若说妄想什么算奢侈
那奢侈就是
想宴飨你的脸庞
不啻一顿豪餐供给

在更清淡的日子,餐桌远逸
眼见清晰
盛载面包屑一粒
心中不由想起你。

816

A Death blow is a Life blow to Some
Who till they died, did not alive become—
Who had they lived, had died but when
They died, Vitality begun.

816①

对有些人而言死的打击就是生的打击
直至死,都未真正活过——
假如活过,也等于死
但当他们死,生命才开始。

---

① 题解:所谓死的打击就是生的打击,意即对方去世的消息,对生者是个活生生的打击。若爱对方而被拒,则活着等于死,及至死去,爱的传奇便开始被传颂,由此开启了新的生命。

817

Given in Marriage unto Thee
Oh thou Celestial Host—
Bride of the Father and the Son
Bride of the Holy Ghost.

Other Betrothal shall dissolve—
Wedlock of Will, decay—
Only the Keeper of this Ring
Conquer Mortality—

817

在婚姻里向你臣服
啊你这上天的主——
圣父和圣子的新娘
圣灵的新娘。

其他的婚约将会解除——
理想中的婚姻，萎枯——
唯有戴这枚戒指的人
超越凡俗——

818

I could not drink it, Sweet,
Till You had tasted first,
Though cooler than the Water was
The Thoughtfullness of Thirst.

818

我不能喝它，亲爱的，
除非你先尝，
虽然比水更凉
是口渴的念想。

819

All I may, if small,
Do it not display
Larger for the Totalness—
'Tis Economy

To bestow a World
And withhold a Star—
Utmost, is Munificence—
Less, tho larger, poor.

819①

我所愿，假如很微小，
就是不要显示
大过全体——
这就叫经济

献出一个世界
留下一颗星星——
至多，算是慷慨——
退一步讲，虽然更大，叫寒碜。

820

All Circumstances are the Frame
In which His Face is set—
All Latitudes exist for His
Sufficient Continent—

The Light His Action, and the Dark
The Leisure of His Will—

---

① 题解：假如我所有的很少，我愿意显示全部，但不要夸大，这就是经济适用的做法；假如拥有很多，献出了全世界，只留下一颗星星，至多被认为是慷慨，或许可能还被认为是寒碜，虽然献出的比前者更多。

In Him Existence serve or set
A Force illegible.

820
所有的环境构成一个框
他的脸被往里放——
所有的地域存在
为了他大陆的富藏——

光明是他在行动,而黑暗
是他意志在闲荡——
存在在他身上提供或注入
一股难以言明的力量。

821
Away from Home are some and I—
An Emigrant to be
In a Metropolis of Homes
Is easy, possibly—

The Habit of a Foreign Sky
We—difficult—acquire
As Children, who remain in Face
The more their Feet retire.

821
我和一些人离开家——
做一个移民迁徙
在无数家园的大都市里
很容易,也许——

活在异域的天空
我们——很难——习惯
就像孩童,脸上无动于衷
双脚已向后退转。

822

This Consciousness that is aware
Of Neighbors and the Sun
Will be the one aware of Death
And that itself alone

Is traversing the interval
Experience between
And most profound experiment
Appointed unto Men—

How adequate unto itself
It's properties shall be
Itself unto itself and none
Shall make discovery.

Adventure most unto itself
The Soul condemned to be—
Attended by a single Hound
It's own identity.

822

感受到邻居和太阳
这一份意识
也会感受到死亡
而且它独自

穿越间隙
一边是体会
一边是最深刻的试验
指定给人类——

它的特性有多胜任

对它自己而言
只有自己露给自己没人
能够发现。

让自己饱尝风雨
灵魂被如此判罚——
由一只猎犬陪同
这身份就是它①。

823

Not that We did, shall be the test
When Act and Will are done
But what Our Lord infers We would
Had We diviner been—

823

并非靠我们已为,作为验证
当行动与意愿完成
而是靠我们的主推断我们意欲何为
假如我们更加神圣——

824

The Wind begun to knead the Grass—
As Women do a Dough—
He flung a Hand full at the Plain—
A Hand full at the Sky—
The Leaves unhooked themselves from Trees—
And started all abroad—
The Dust did scoop itself like Hands—
And throw away the Road—

---

① 这身份就是它(It's own identity):指猎犬就是它(灵魂)自己,两者同一(identity)。

The Wagons—quickened on the Street—
The Thunders gossiped low—
The Lightning showed a Yellow Head—
And then a livid Toe—
The Birds put up the Bars to Nests—
The Cattle flung to Barns—
Then came one drop of Giant Rain—
And then, as if the Hands
That held the Dams—had parted hold—
The Waters Wrecked the Sky—
But overlooked my Father's House—
Just Quartering a Tree—

(first version)

The Wind begun to rock the Grass
With threatening Tunes and low—
He threw a Menace at the Earth—
A Menace at the Sky.

The Leaves unhooked themselves from Trees—
And started all abroad
The Dust did scoop itself like Hands
And threw away the Road.

The Wagons quickened on the Streets
The Thunder hurried slow—
The Lightning showed a Yellow Beak
And then a livid Claw.

The Birds put up the Bars to Nests—
The Cattle fled to Barns—
There came one drop of Giant Rain
And then as if the Hands

That held the Dams had parted hold
The Waters Wrecked the Sky,
But overlooked my Father's House—
Just quartering a Tree—

(second version)

824
风开始揉捏草——
像妇女揉捏面团——
他挥舞一只手在草原——
另一只手在天上——
叶子纷纷从树上脱落——
开始外出漂泊——
尘土像用手将自己舀起——
在大道上播撒出去——
四轮马车——在大街上疾驰——
雷霆低语——
闪电现出一个黄色的头——
然后是一只乌青的脚趾——
鸟儿拴上巢门——
牛奔回牛棚——
此时天空落下大雨的一滴——
随后，好似
支撑大坝的手——放开——
洪水漫过天空——
但避开了我父亲的房屋——
仅摧断了一棵树——

（第一个版本）

风开始摇晃草
以吓人的低低的曲调——
他向大地发出恐吓——
也向天空发出威胁。

叶子纷纷从树上脱落——
开始外出漂泊
尘土像用手将自己舀起
在大道上播撒出去。

四轮马车在大街上疾驰
雷霆似急又缓——
闪电现出一个黄色的喙
然后是一只乌青的爪。

鸟儿拴上巢门——
牛逃回牛棚——
此时天空落下大雨的一滴
随后好似

支撑大坝的手放开
洪水漫过天空,
但避开了我父亲的房屋——
仅摧断了一棵树——

(第二个版本)

825

An Hour is a Sea
Between a few, and me—
With them would Harbor be—

825①

一小时是大海一片

---

① 本诗是狄金森 1865 年 12 月初写给嫂子苏珊的一封信中的结尾。诗的前面是这样的话:"I am glad you go – It does not remove you. I seek you first in Amherst, then turn my thoughts without a Whip – so well they follow you – "(L312)当时苏珊住在纽约的妹妹玛莎(Martha Smith)那里。诗歌表达了狄金森渴望和苏珊以及其他几个好朋友在一起的心情,她们之间一小时的分离,对于她而言,就像间隔了一片大海之宽。狄金森和她们在一起的感觉仿佛是在港湾里面一样自在和安全。

就在那少数几个，与我之间——
和他们在一起就像在港湾里面①——

826

Love reckons by itself—alone—
"As large as I" —relate the Sun
To One who never felt it blaze—
Itself is all the like it has—

826

爱只能——拿自己把自己衡量——
"像我一般大"——太阳讲
对从未感受它烈焰的人——
它只能以自己为准绳——

827

The Only News I know
Is Bulletins all Day
From Immortality.

The Only Shows I see—
Tomorrow and Today—
Perchance Eternity—

The Only One I meet
Is God—The Only Street—
Existence—This traversed

If Other News there be—
Or Admirabler Show—
I'll tell it You—

---

① 和他们在一起就像在港湾里面（With them would Harbor be）；或也可译为"港湾可能在他们那边"。

827①

我唯一知道的消息
都在每天的新闻公告里
来自永生。

我唯一见过的表演——
是今天和明天——
也许还有永恒——

我唯一邂逅的那位
是上帝——那条唯一的街——
存在——穿越它

如果还有其他消息——
或更精彩的表演——
我会告诉你——

828

The Robin is the One
That interrupt the Morn
With hurried—few—express Reports
When March is scarcely on—

---

① 本诗第一节是艾米莉·狄金森1864年6月初写给文学导师希金森的一封回信的一部分。当时狄金森正在马萨诸塞州的剑桥治疗眼疾,住在剑桥东边4英里外的波士顿的两位表妹弗朗西丝·诺克罗斯和路易莎·诺克罗斯家里。此前她接到希金森的信,信中希金森说他在美国南北战争(1861—1865)中受了伤(1862年8月),狄金森在这封回信的开头说:"Are you in danger – I did not know that you were hurt. Will you tell me more? Mr Hawthorne died. I was ill since September, and since April, in Boston, for a Physician's care – He does not let me go, yet I work in my Prison, and make Guests for myself – … I wish to see you more than before I failed – Will you tell me your health? I am surprised and anxious, since receiving your note – "然后紧接本诗第一节。在信的结尾,狄金森写道:"Knowledge of your recovery – would excel my own – "(L290)。另参见第617首和第684首诗的注释。

The Robin is the One
That overflow the Noon
With her cherubic quantity—
An April but begun—

The Robin is the One
That speechless from her Nest
Submit that Home—and Certainty
And Sanctity, are best

828
就是那只知更鸟
它一大早就叫
急匆匆——用三言两语——迅速报告
当三月才刚来到——

就是那只知更鸟
让正午充溢
它天使般的声音——
四月才刚开始——

就是那只知更鸟
在巢中一言不发
主张家园——还有安定
以及圣洁，才是最佳

829
Ample make this Bed—
Make this Bed with Awe—
In it wait till Judgment break
Excellent and Fair.

Be it's Mattress straight—
Be it's Pillow round—
Let no Sunrise' yellow noise
Interrupt this Ground—

829①

把这张床做得宽敞——
做这张床怀着敬畏——
在里面等到审判宣布
公正又完美。

让它的床垫平直——
让它的枕头圆鼓——
别让日出黄色的噪音
侵扰这块乐土——

830

To this World she returned.
But with a tinge of that—
A Compound manner,
As a Sod
Espoused a Violet,
That chiefer to the Skies
Than to himself, allied,
Dwelt hesitating, half of Dust,
And half of Day, the Bride.

---

① 艾米莉·狄金森在1883年4月写给朋友耐尔斯（Thomas Niles, 1825—1894）的一封信中附寄了本诗，并给本诗起标题为"乡村葬礼"（Country Burial）。

830①
她重回这个世界。
但带有那个世界的气息——
一种混合的样子,
像一块草皮②
娶了一株紫罗兰,
但更似与天宇
胜过与他③,联姻,
这新娘,栖居而犹豫,
半属尘土,半属白日。

831

Dying! To be afraid of thee
One must to thine Artillery
Have left exposed a Friend—
Than thine old Arrow is a Shot
Delivered straighter to the Heart
The leaving Love behind.

Not for itself, the Dust is shy,
But, enemy, Beloved be
Thy Batteries divorce.
Fight sternly in a Dying eye
Two Armies, Love and Certainty
And Love and the Reverse.

---

① 本诗写于1864年夏天。1864年3月20日,范德比尔特太太(Mrs. Gertrude Lefferts Vanderbilt)因听到痛苦的惨叫声来到后门,却意外地被一颗本该打中她的女仆的手枪子弹打倒,射击人是她女仆的疯狂追求者。范德比尔特太太受重伤后最终痊愈,此事打动了艾米莉·狄金森,她由此送给范德比尔特太太两首诗,即本诗和下一首(第831首)诗。本诗写明是送给"Mrs. Gertrude",根据诗的内容,是欢迎对方从鬼门关重返人间。

② 草皮(Sod):关于Sod和Violet,见于狄金森信件中:"the new violet sucking her way among the sods"(L203)。另见第392首诗:"Through the Dark Sod – as Education –/ The Lily passes sure – "。

③ 他(himself):应是指"Sod"。上一行的主语应是紫罗兰。

831①

即将死去！要害怕你
须向你的大炮献礼
献上一位朋友——
一发炮弹比你的旧箭
更径直射入心间
留下的爱在身后。

尘土羞怯，非因它自己，
而是，死敌，亲爱无比
被你的排炮拆散。
不屈地战斗于垂死的眼睛
有两支军队，爱与确定
以及爱与相反。

832

Soto! Explore thyself!
Therein thyself shalt find
The "Undiscovered Continent" —
No Settler had the Mind.

832

索托②！探索你自己！
在你那里你会找到

---

① 这是艾米莉·狄金森送给1864年3月20日受枪伤的范德比尔特太太的两首诗中的一首（另一首是第830首）。诗的大意为：人将死，这是令人害怕的，不过那是因为人（范德比尔特太太）主动送到了大炮（枪）口上，炮弹自然比旧时的箭更致命，但死者的爱留在了身后（人间）。尘土自然有些羞怯，不是因为自己而羞怯，而是尘土要接收的所谓大炮的死敌，其实也是亲爱无比的亲人（即 a Friend），只是被大炮拆离了。可以看到在被大炮（枪）击中而即将死去的人的眼里，交集着两种想法，一种是爱和确定，即将死者确定她含爱死去后，留在身后的人间仍充满爱；另一种是爱与不确定，即含爱死去的将死者无法确定她身后的世界是否仍充满爱。

② 索托（Soto）：赫尔南多·德·索托（Hernando de Soto 1496—1542），西班牙探险家，他的探险足迹主要分布在美洲，尤其是北美。

那"未被发现的陆地"——
没一个定居者有这头脑。

833

Perhaps you think me stooping
I'm not ashamed of that
Christ—stooped until He touched the Grave—
Do those at Sacrament

Commemorate Dishonor
Or love annealed of love
Until it bend as low as Death
Redignified, above?

833

也许你认为我在弯腰求全
但我并不觉丢脸
基督也弯腰——直至他触到坟墓——
圣礼上的那些人物

是纪念不名誉事件
或是爱经过爱的淬炼
直至它躬身低如死亡
在上界,能重获尊严?

834

Before He comes we weigh the Time!
'Tis Heavy and 'tis Light.
When He depart, an Emptiness
Is the prevailing Freight.

834

他来之前我们称量时间!

它既沉重又轻浅。
当他离开,虚空
这货品最常见。

835

Nature and God—I neither knew
Yet Both so well knew me
They startled, like Executors
Of My identity.

Yet Neither told—that I could learn—
My Secret as secure
As Herschel's private interest
Or Mercury's affair—

835

大自然和上帝——我都不认识
但我对于他们俩却是熟人
像两位执行者,他们感到惊奇
对我的身份。

但都不告诉我——我有权知道——
我的秘密如此严实
像赫歇尔①的个人爱好

---

① 赫歇尔(Herschel):Sir Frederick William Herschel(1738—1822),英国天文学家,出生于德国汉诺威,1757年移民英国。他于1781年发现了天王星(Uranus),因此一夜成名,被英王乔治三世(George Ⅲ,1738—1820)任命为 Court Astronomer。他后来被选为英国皇家学会会员(Fellow of the Royal Society),是1820年皇家天文学会(the Royal Astronomical Society)成立时的第一任主席。

或墨丘利神①的大事——

836
Truth—is as old as God—
His Twin identity
And will endure as long as He
A Co-Eternity—

And perish on the Day
Himself is borne away
From Mansion of the Universe
A lifeless Deity.

836②
真理——古老如上帝——
论身份是他的孪生
并长期和上帝一起
忍受同样的永恒——

并会在那一天消弭
当他被抬起
离开宇宙的宅第
像一个无生命的神祇。

837
How well I knew Her not
Whom not to know has been

---

① 墨丘利（Mercury）：罗马神话中主掌贸易、旅行、雄辩、偷盗之神，是主神朱庇特（Jupiter）和女神迈亚（Maia）之子，脚穿带翅膀的便鞋，左手持节杖（caduceus），为诸神的信使。在希腊神话中称为赫耳墨斯（Hermes），是主神宙斯（Zeus）和女神迈亚（Maia）之子，是奥林匹亚诸神的信使。在奥林匹亚十二神中，他是除酒神狄俄尼索斯（Dionysus，即罗马神话中的Bacchus）之外年纪最小的神。

② 参阅第449首诗，狄金森将真理与美相比拟。

A Bounty in prospective, now
Next Door to mine the Pain.

837①
我对她很不熟悉
不认识反而一直激起
丰富的想象,如今
我的隔壁满是悲戚。

838
Impossibility, like Wine
Exhilirates the Man
Who tastes it; Possibility
Is flavorless—Combine

A Chance's faintest Tincture
And in the former Dram
Enchantment makes ingredient
As certainly as Doom—

838
不可能,就像酒
让品尝的人
兴奋;可能
没滋味——混合

机会的一丁点印迹
加上前者的一小滴

---

① 这是艾米莉·狄金森1864年写给朋友玛利亚(Maria Whitney,1830—1910)的诗。玛利亚的妹妹萨拉(Sarah Whitney)于1864年7月9日死于康涅狄格州的普利茅斯镇(Plymouth, Connecticut)。

这成分就能产生魔力
如死亡般确定无疑——

839

Always Mine!
No more Vacation!
Term of Light this Day begun!
Failless as the fair rotation
Of the Seasons and the Sun.

Old the Grace, but new the Subjects—
Old, indeed, the East,
Yet upon His Purple Programme
Every Dawn, is first.

839

永远属于我!
不再有假期!
光的学期今天开始!
准时无虞
像四季和太阳美丽的轮替。

光耀依旧,但课程加了新意——
东方,确实,也与往时无二,
但在他紫色的课程表里
每个黎明,都是第一课。

840

I cannot buy it—'tis not sold—
There is no other in the World—
Mine was the only one

I was so happy I forgot

To shut the Door And it went out
And I am all alone—

If I could find it Anywhere
I would not mind the journey there
Though it took all my store

But just to look it in the Eye—
"Did'st thou?" "Thou did'st not mean," to say,
Then, turn my Face away.

840
我无法买到它——它不供出售——
世界别的地方都没有——
我的这个是唯一

我很高兴我忘记
关门然后它就逃逸
然后仅剩我自己——

如果我知道它在某地
我不介意跟随到那里
即使耗尽我所有的积蓄

但只为盯着它的眼——
说,"是你?""你并非故意,"
然后,就将我的脸转移。

841
A Moth the hue of this
Haunts Candles in Brazil.
Nature's Experience would make
Our Reddest Second pale.

Nature is fond, I sometimes think,
Of Trinkets, as a Girl.

841①
这种颜色的飞蛾
在巴西围着烛光飞。
大自然的经验会让
我们最火红的刹那变得苍白。

我有时想,大自然,
喜欢小饰物,像个女孩。

842
Good to hide, and hear 'em hunt!
Better, to be found,
If one care to, that is,
The Fox fits the Hound—

Good to know, and not tell,
Best, to know and tell,
Can one find the rare Ear
Not too dull—

842
藏起来真好,听他们来找!
最好,被找到,
如果愿意,也就是说,
狐狸符合猎狗的需要——

知道真好,且隐而不讲,
最好,知道就讲,

---

① 第541首诗提到巴西的蝴蝶。

假如能碰上难得的耳朵
不太迷惘——

843

I made slow Riches but my Gain
Was steady as the Sun
And every Night, it numbered more
Than the preceding One

All Days, I did not earn the same
But my perceiveless Gain
Inferred the less by Growing than
The Sum that it had grown.

843

我慢慢积攒财富但我的收入
稳定如太阳
每一晚,它都增加
相比于前一晚的数量

每天,我所得不一
但我那无形的收入
估计增长的较少
相比于那已增长的总数。

844

Spring is the Period
Express from God.
Among the other seasons
Himself abide,

But during March and April
None stir abroad

Without a cordial interview
With God.

844
春季是一段时期
由上帝献出。
在其他季节里
他自己停驻,

但在三月和四月间
没人在外喧闹
如果还没和上帝
好好聊一聊。

845
Be Mine the Doom—
Sufficient Fame—
To perish in Her Hand!

845
毁灭为我所有——
这名头已足够——
命丧她手!

846
Twice had Summer her fair Verdure
Proffered to the Plain—
Twice a Winter's silver Fracture
On the Rivers been—

Two full Autumns for the Squirrel
Bounteous prepared—
Nature, Had'st thou not a Berry
For thy wandering Bird?

846

已经两次夏季给原野
献出她美丽的青翠——
已经两次冬季在河面
洒下碎裂的银灰——

两个丰盈的秋季
为松鼠准备了富饶——
大自然,你就没有一颗浆果
给你漂泊的小鸟?

847

Finite—to fail, but infinite to Venture—
For the one ship that struts the shore
Many's the gallant—overwhelmed Creature
Nodding in Navies nevermore—

847

失败——有限,但冒险无限——
相对于那艘在海滨雄赳赳的船
有许多英勇的——被淹没的生灵
再没机会在舰队里把头点——

848

Just as He spoke it from his Hands
This Edifice remain—
A Turret more, a Turret less
Dishonor his Design—

According as his skill prefer
It perish, or endure—

Content, soe'er, it ornament
His absent character.

848
正如他所言出自他的手
这座大厦得以屹立——
多一个角楼,少一个角楼
都会玷污他的设计——

鉴于他技艺的偏好
它消失,或维持——
都满意,不论如何,已粉饰
他不在场的性质。

849
The good Will of a Flower
The Man who would possess
Must first present
Certificate
Of minted Holiness.

849
一朵花的美好心愿
是拥有者
必先
出示证件
表明被认可的圣洁。

850
I sing to use the Waiting
My Bonnet but to tie
And shut the Door unto my House
No more to do have I

Till His best step approaching
We journey to the Day
And tell each other how We sung
To Keep the Dark away.

850
我用等待的时间歌唱
我的软帽已系上
也关闭了屋房
不再有什么可忙

直至他美妙的脚步近身旁
我们一起往那一天闯荡①
告诉对方我们曾如何歌唱
为把黑暗阻挡②。

851
When the Astronomer stops seeking
For his Pleiad's Face—
When the lone British Lady
Forsakes the Arctic Race

When to his Covenant Needle
The Sailor doubting turns—
It will be amply early
To ask what treason means.

---

① 我们一起往那一天闯荡（We journey to the Day）：原文中"the Day"可以理解为"the Day of Judgement"等，则本诗说话者有明确的目的地。或译"我们一起在白天游荡"，则本诗中说话者没有明确的目的地。

② 艾米莉·狄金森在1862年4月25日写给文学导师希金森的第二封信里有这样的说法："I had a terror – since September – I could tell to none – and so I sing, as the Boy does by the Burying Ground – because I am afraid – "（L261）

851①

当那位天文学家不再探寻
昴宿星的脸——
当那位孤单的英国女士②
放弃北极探险

当根据他惯常使用的指南针
水手满腹狐疑地调转船——
现在还太早去追问
什么是背叛。

852

Apology for Her
Be rendered by the Bee—
Herself, without a Parliament
Apology for Me.

852

为她辩护
由蜜蜂说出——
她自己，未经商议③
就为我辩护。

853

When One has given up One's life
The parting with the rest
Feels easy, as when Day lets go

---

① 关于背叛（treason），另参见第1410首也提到"Treason"，还有人名"Katie"；第23首提到"Pleiad"和"traitor"。

② 英国人富兰克林（Sir John Franklin, 1786—1847）1845年开启他最后一次北极探险，一去不回。其夫人（Lady Jane Franklin）随后10年资助搜救队前往北极地区搜救，直至1858年才确认其丈夫已于1847年遇难。

③ 商议（Parliament）：也可译为"发言人""代言人"。

Entirely the West

The Peaks, that lingered last
Remain in Her regret
As scarcely as the Iodine
Upon the Cataract.

853
当一个人将生命放弃
与他人别离
感觉很容易,就像白昼完全抽身离去
自天空以西

群峰,徘徊到最后
沉浸于她的悲伤
几乎不像那紫红
弥漫在瀑布上方。

854
Banish Air from Air—
Divide Light if you dare—
They'll meet
While Cubes in a Drop
Or Pellets of Shape
Fit
Films cannot annul
Odors return whole
Force Flame
And with a Blonde push
Over your impotence
Flits Steam.

854
将空气从空气里驱赶——
把光分开如果你够大胆——
他们还会相遇
只要水滴中的立方体
或有形的小球体
相契
水雾无法消除
香味返回全部
强大的火力
只需淡黄色的一推
在你的无能之上
水蒸气逃逸。

855
To own the Art within the Soul
The Soul to entertain
With Silence as a Company
And Festival maintain

Is an unfurnished Circumstance
Possession is to One
As an Estate perpetual
Or a reduceless Mine.

855
在灵魂里拥有
娱乐灵魂的艺术
与寂静为伍
却日日庆祝

是一种未完备的情景
拥有对人而言

像一处永久地产
或一座永不贬值的矿山。

856

There is a finished feeling
Experienced at Graves—
A leisure of the Future—
A Wilderness of Size.

By Death's bold Exhibition
Preciser what we are
And the Eternal function
Enabled to infer.

856

有一种解脱的感觉
在墓园里体验——
一种未来的悠闲——
一种规模的荒原。

通过死亡的大胆展示
更清楚我们自己
而那永恒的意义
由此可以推理。

857

Uncertain lease—develops lustre
On Time
Uncertain Grasp, appreciation
Of Sum—

The shorter Fate—is oftener the chiefest
Because

Inheritors upon a tenure
Prize—

857

不明确的租约——给时间
镀上光芒
不明确的理解，让人渴望
把全部欣赏——

越短暂的命运——越往往是最重要
因为
这段命运的承受者
觉得弥足珍贵——

858

This Chasm, Sweet, upon my life
I mention it to you,
When Sunrise through a fissure drop
The Day must follow too.

If we demur, it's gaping sides
Disclose as 'twere a Tomb
Ourself am lying straight wherein
The Favorite of Doom.

When it has just contained a Life
Then, Darling, it will close
And yet so bolder every Day
So turbulent it grows

I'm tempted half to stitch it up
With a remaining Breath
I should not miss in yielding, though

To Him, it would be Death—

And so I bear it big about
My Burial—before
A Life quite ready to depart
Can harass me no more—

858①
爱人,我生命中,这个裂口
我告诉给你,
当朝阳透过一条裂缝坠落
白昼也会随之而去。

如果我们意见不一,它洞开的两壁
显示如一个墓室
我们就直挺挺躺在
死亡至爱之地。

当它容纳了一个生命
随后,亲爱的,它就合上
然而它每天仍如此张狂
如此激荡

我有点想把裂口缝上
用尚存的一口气息
在放弃时不应忘记,虽然
对于他,仍是必死无疑——

---

① 题解:爱是一个伤口,我们意见不一时伤口会扩大如墓室,会带来死亡。但即使其中一人心死了,墓室闭合,但依然无法过得安宁,依然激荡不安,令人几乎窒息。临死前告诫自己,不要忘记用最后一丝力气,把爱的裂口缝上,虽然最后也仍是死。为此"我"携着巨大的裂口,到"我"的埋葬地。我这样一个行将离去的生命,不会再对什么依依不舍了。

所以我携着它很显眼
到我的埋葬地——面前
一个已准备离去的生命
不会再令我梦萦魂牵——

859

A doubt if it be Us
Assists the staggering Mind
In an extremer Anguish
Until it footing find.

An Unreality is lent,
A merciful Mirage
That makes the living possible
While it suspends the lives.

859

假如我们疑虑
会有益于震惊的头脑
在更大的痛苦里
找到落脚。

一种非现实得以借出,
一幅仁慈的蜃景
让生活变得可能
虽然它冻结了生命。

860

Absence disembodies—so does Death
Hiding individuals from the Earth
Superposition helps, as well as love—
Tenderness decreases as we prove—

860①

缺席制造无形——死亡亦如是
让诸多个体从地球隐匿
迷信会有用,爱也可以——
一旦我们经历,柔情就会减低——

861

Split the Lark—and you'll find the Music—
Bulb after Bulb, in Silver rolled—
Scantilly dealt to the Summer Morning
Saved for your Ear when Lutes be old.

Loose the Flood—you shall find it patent—
Gush after Gush, reserved for you—
Scarlet Experiment! Sceptic Thomas!
Now, do you doubt that your Bird was true?

861

剖开云雀——你会发现音乐——
一波接一波滚动,像银球——
几乎无关夏日的早晨
专为你耳朵准备,当诗琴已老朽。

释放那洪流——你会发现它涌出——
一汩接一汩,都是为你留存——

---

① 题解:缺席和死亡一样,都令存在不在场,不现形体。要使诸多个体从地球上隐匿,可以通过迷信或爱,想象不在眼前的人在彼岸或天堂如何如何,不过一旦真有了这个经历,则也令想象者明白被想象者已不在现场,对其柔情自然也减低了。本诗写于 1864 年(富兰克林版认为是 1865 年)。狄金森 1866 年 5 月初写给霍兰夫人(Mrs. J. G. Holland, 即 Elizabeth Chapin Holland, 1823—1896)的一封信中有这样的表述:"When you had gone the love came. I supposed it would. The supper of the heart is when the guest has gone."(L318)

猩红的试验！疑虑的多马①！
现在，你还怀疑你鸟儿的情真？

862

Light is sufficient to itself—
If Others want to see
It can be had on Window Panes
Some Hours in the Day.

But not for Compensation—
It holds as large a Glow
To Squirrel in the Himmaleh
Precisely, as to you.

862

光已自我满足——
如果有人想要一见
它显现于玻璃窗户
好几个小时，在白天。

但非为获得弥补——
它以巨大的绚丽

---

① 多马（Thomas）：《圣经·新约·约翰福音》第 20 章第 24～28 节记载，耶稣死后复活，来到门徒中间向门徒说话，但十二门徒之一的多马当时不在场，他于是不信耶稣复活，又过了八日，耶稣再次来到门徒中间，多马摸了耶稣有钉痕的手和肋旁，终于相信耶稣复活了。"But Thomas, one of the twelve, called Didymus, was not with them when Jesus came. The other disciples therefore said unto him, We have seen the LORD. But he said unto them, Except I shall see in his hands the print of the nails, and put my finger into the print of the nails, and thrust my hand into his side, I will not believe. And after eight days again his disciples were within, and Thomas with them: then came Jesus, the doors being shut, and stood in the midst, and said, Peace be unto you. Then saith he to Thomas, Reach hither thy finger, and behold my hands; and reach hither thy hand, and thrust it into my side: and be not faithless, but believing. And Thomas answered and said unto him, My LORD and my God."（John 20: 24 - 28）另见第 555 首诗中也提到多马。

光耀喜马拉雅山的松鼠
准确地说,也光耀着你。

863

That Distance was between Us
That is not of Mile or Main—
The Will it is that situates—
Equator—never can—

863

我们之间的距离
不是沧海或大道——
位于其间的是意志——
赤道——绝对办不到——

864

The Robin for the Crumb
Returns no syllable
But long records the Lady's name
In Silver Chronicle.

864①

知更鸟不为那些碎食
回报一声辛苦
唯长久铭记那女士的名字
在银色的史簿。

865

He outstripped Time with but a Bout,
He outstripped Stars and Sun

---

① 关于鸟儿对面包屑的感激,另参阅第760首。

And then, unjaded, challenged God
In presence of the Throne.

And He and He in mighty List
Unto this present, run,
The larger Glory for the less
A just sufficient Ring.

865①

他轻而易举超过时间，
还超过星星和太阳
然后，毫无倦意，向上帝挑战
在王座面前。

然后他和他就雄赳赳地排列
向着当前，奔跑，
以较大的荣耀换取较小的
一枚名副其实的胜利指环。

866

Fame is the tint that Scholars leave
Upon their Setting Names—
The Iris not of Occident
That disappears as comes—

866

名声是那色彩
学者们置于他们陨落的名字——

---

① 题解："他"一发力就超过时间，还超过了星星和太阳，在天堂的王座面前直接向上帝挑战。他俩以当前为目标的赛跑是从天堂奔向人间的比赛，是以较大荣耀换取较小荣耀的比赛，奖赏虽只是一枚胜利指环，却已足够。本诗第二节也可有其他解读，尤其是对 present、the less 以及 Ring 等词的理解。

那鸢尾花①不像西天
一来就消失——

867

Escaping backward to perceive
The Sea upon our place—
Escaping forward, to confront
His glittering Embrace—

Retreating up, a Billow's height
Retreating blinded down
Our undermining feet to meet
Instructs to the Divine.

867②

向后逃会看见
大海把我们领地笼罩——
向前逃，会直面
它闪亮的拥抱——

向上退，达到巨浪之高
向下盲目退去
碰到我们日渐虚弱的双脚
引向那神圣之域。

868

They ask but our Delight—

---

① 鸢尾花（The Iris）：此植物开大瓣斑斓的白、黄或紫的花。此行和下一行指鸢尾花的色彩不像西天日落时的色彩那样，刚一出现就消失，喻指名声如鸢尾花一样，是长久的，不是短暂的。原文"Iris"也可指希腊神话中的彩虹女神，为诸神的信使（the Greek goddess of the rainbow and a messenger of the gods）。

② 题解：在生活的大海上，逃无可逃，只能走向神圣之域，皈依上帝。

The Darlings of the Soil
And grant us all their Countenance
For a penurious smile.

868①
它们只要求我们快乐——
那些泥土的相好
并许给我们全部的娇容
为一个清寒的微笑。

869
Because the Bee may blameless hum
For Thee a Bee do I become
List even unto Me.

Because the Flowers unafraid
May lift a look on thine, a Maid
Alway a Flower would be.

Nor Robins, Robins need not hide
When Thou upon their Crypts intrude
So Wings bestow on Me
Or Petals, or a Dower of Buzz
That Bee to ride, or Flower of Furze
I that way worship Thee.

---

① 题解：只要我们给予那些花朵一个无须付出多大努力的笑容，它们就全都向我们绽放。

869①
因为蜜蜂可以不受指责随意嗡嗡
我就为你变成一只蜜蜂
请静静听我歌唱。

因为花儿可以不必顾忌
可以抬眼望你,一位少女
愿永远变成花儿的模样。

知更鸟也不惧,知更鸟无须藏匿
当你闯入它们幽密领地
所以请赐给我翅膀
或花瓣,或嗡鸣的才华
蜜蜂可以驾驭,或荆豆花
我就那样对你景仰。

870
Finding is the first Act
The second, loss,
Third, Expedition for
The "Golden Fleece"

Fourth, no Discovery—
Fifth, no Crew—
Finally, no Golden Fleece—
Jason—sham—too.

---

① 本诗中的"我"愿意为"你"变成蜜蜂、花朵和知更鸟,以便可以像他们那样接近"你",景仰"你"。但在狄金森 1856 年 8 月初写给霍兰夫人的一封信中则表示庆幸对方不是玫瑰、蜜蜂和知更鸟,因为它们都将很快离去:"I'm so glad you are not a blossom, for those in my garden fade, and then a 'reaper whose name is Death' has come to get a few to help him make a bouquet for himself, so I'm glad you are not a rose – and I'm glad you are not a bee, for where they go when summer's done, only the thyme knows, and even were you a robin, when the west winds came, you would coolly wink at me, and away, some morning!"(L185)

870

第一幕是找到
第二，失掉，
第三，远征寻找
那"金羊毛"①

第四，无任何发现——
第五，没看到船员——
最后，没找到金羊毛——
连伊阿宋②——也只是——传言。

871

The Sun and Moon must make their haste—
The Stars express around
For in the Zones of Paradise
The Lord alone is burned—

His Eye, it is the East and West—
The North and South when He
Do concentrate His Countenance
Like Glow Worms, flee away—

Oh Poor and Far—
Oh Hindred Eye
That hunted for the Day—
The Lord a Candle entertains
Entirely for Thee—

---

① 金羊毛（Golden Fleece）：一只身上长有双翼、羊皮为纯金的公羊的毛，是权力（authority）和王位（kingship）的象征。
② 伊阿宋（Jason）：伊阿宋是古希腊神话中的英雄，古希腊塞萨利（Thessaly）地区城邦国家爱俄尔卡斯（Iolcus）的国工埃宋（Aeson）的儿子，他是黑海边的城邦国家科尔喀斯（Colchis，现今格鲁吉亚一地区）的国王埃厄忒斯（Aeetes）的女儿——女巫美狄亚（Medea）的丈夫。伊阿宋带领航船阿尔戈号（Argo）上的阿尔戈英雄们（Argonauts）历经千辛万苦前往科尔喀斯（Colchis）寻找金羊毛（Golden Fleece）。

871①

太阳和月亮一定要赶快——
群星在四周匆匆显现
因为在天堂那一带
只有主被点燃——

他的眼,西和东——
以及南和北
当他专注自己的面容
就都像萤火虫,逃离无影踪——

啊,可怜又遥远——
啊,受阻的眼
在找寻白天——
主守着一根蜡烛
全心等候你——

872

As the Starved Maelstrom laps the Navies
As the Vulture teased
Forces the Broods in lonely Valleys
As the Tiger eased

By but a Crumb of Blood, fasts Scarlet
Till he meet a Man
Dainty adorned with Veins and Tissues
And partakes—his Tongue

---

① 题解:日月星辰要赶紧展现自己的威力,因为到了天堂那里,就只有主的眼被点燃,发出光,就没有日月星辰展现自己的份了。连地球的东南西北四轴,在主专注于自己的面容时,都像萤火虫一样逃逸了。不过主并非全无怜悯之心,他守着一根蜡烛,等待那些贫苦可怜的遥远的人,那些有眼疾却寻觅光明的人!

Cooled by the Morsel for a moment
Grows a fiercer thing
Till he esteem his Dates and Cocoa
A Nutrition mean

I, of a finer Famine
Deem my Supper dry
For but a Berry of Domingo
And a Torrid Eye.

872
像饥饿的大漩涡将舰队吞下肚
像秃鹫戏弄
把雏鸟赶入偏僻的山谷
像老虎变得从容

只因一点血迹,禁食腥红
直至他遇见一个人
浑身突显诱人血管和肌肉
于是吞食——他的舌头

因一小口才缓和了一下
就变成更猛烈的样子
以至于认为大枣和椰子①
都是粗食

我,怀有更深的饥饿
觉得晚餐乏味没劲
只有一枚浆果来自多明各
和一只热烈的眼睛。

---

① 椰子(Cocoa):指 coco 或 coconut,即椰子。

873

Ribbons of the Year—
Multitude Brocade—
Worn to Nature's Party once

Then, as flung aside
As a faded Bead
Or a Wrinkled Pearl——
Who shall charge the Vanity
Of the Maker's Girl?

873①

流年的飘带——
缤纷的锦缎——
曾被披戴参加大自然的盛会

随后,就被弃置一边
像一颗褪色的念珠
或一颗起皱的珍珠——
谁会去指责
造物主的女儿虚荣无度?

874

They won't frown always—some sweet Day
When I forget to tease—
They'll recollect how cold I looked
And how I just said "Please."

---

① 题注:大自然四季缤纷,但轮转更替,不论花开花落,既荣再枯,都是短暂的美丽,可是有谁会去指责这造物主的女儿爱慕虚荣?

Then They will hasten to the Door
To call the little Girl
Who cannot thank Them for the Ice
That filled the lisping full.

874①

他们不会总是皱眉——某个甜美的日子
当我忘记逗趣——
他们会记起我曾经表情多冷冰
只会说一个"请"字。

然后他们会赶到门口
去唤那小女孩
她无法对他们言谢
满嘴的冰粒咿呀难开。

875

I stepped from Plank to Plank
A slow and cautious way
The Stars about my Head I felt
About my Feet the Sea.

I knew not but the next
Would be my final inch—
This gave me that precarious Gait
Some call Experience.

---

① 题解:"我"喜欢逗趣、取笑,并不讨"他们"喜欢,但我这一特点并非总令他们皱眉。某个美好的日子,当"他们"没听到我的逗趣声,会突然想起刚才"我"看起来很冷,话语不多只会说一个"请",表达拜托或求救,然后才赶到门口唤"我",发现"我"满嘴是冰,已冻得口齿不清,无法逗趣。纵如此,"我"也不会感谢"他们"。

875

我从一块木板迈向一块木板
一副缓慢小心的姿态
我感觉头上是星星
脚下是大海。

我不知下一块会不会
是我最后的一寸之地①——
这令我的步法岌岌可危
有人称之为经历。

876

It was a Grave, yet bore no Stone
Enclosed 'twas not of Rail
A Consciousness it's Acre, and
It held a Human Soul.

Entombed by whom, for what offence
If Home or Foreign born—
Had I the curiosity
'Twere not appeased of men

Till Resurrection, I must guess
Denied the small desire
A Rose upon it's Ridge to sow
Or take away a Briar.

876

这是一座坟墓,但没一块石头
也不用围栏围住

---

① 最后的一寸之地(final inch):据 *Emily Dickinson Lexicon*,final inch 可指 death、last breath。

大小全由人感悟,而且
有个人类的灵魂居住。

由谁埋入,犯了什么罪
出生在国外或国内——
纵然我有这好奇
也无法将人心抚慰

直至复活日,我还得猜
将我的小欲望压抑
在墓脊上栽一株玫瑰
或除去一根荆棘。

877
Each Scar I'll keep for Him
Instead I'll say of Gem
In His long Absence worn
A Costlier one

But every Tear I bore
Were He to count them o'er
His own would fall so more
I'll mis sum them.

877①
每个疤痕我会为他留存
相反我称其为宝石
他长期不在的日子
我戴更贵重的一粒

---

① 题解:长期分离,令爱受伤,但"我"会将它们一一留存,并视之为宝石,且贵过宝石。假如"他"知道我流泪,"他"会流得更多,因此,我必要错计我流泪的总数,以免对方伤心更多。

但我含的每一颗泪滴
假如他全部计数
他自己会流得更多
我要错计总数。

878

The Sun is gay or stark
According to our Deed.
If Merry, He is merrier—
If eager for the Dead

Or an expended Day
He helped to make too bright
His mighty pleasure suits Us not
It magnifies our Freight

878

太阳愉悦还是绷脸
就看我们的表现。
如果我们快乐,他更快乐——
如果渴望死者

或某个耗尽的日子
他帮着使之太过绚烂
他巨大的欢乐于我们不宜
反而增大我们的负担

879

Each Second is the last
Perhaps, recalls the Man
Just measuring unconsciousness
The Sea and Spar between.

To fail within a Chance—
How terribler a thing
Than perish from the Chance's list
Before the Perishing!

879

每一刻都是最后一刻
或许,那个人的忆念
只是感受冥寂
在大海与桅杆之间。

在一次机遇中失败——
更令人怅惘
比起连机遇的名单都没登上
就直接消亡!

880

The Bird must sing to earn the Crumb
What merit have the Tune
No Breakfast if it guaranty

The Rose content may bloom
To gain renown of Lady's Drawer
But if the Lady come
But once a Century, the Rose
Superfluous become—

880

鸟儿必须歌唱以挣得面包粒
乐曲有何意义
如果不能确保将早餐换取

玫瑰会由衷绽放自己

以获得进入女士抽屉的荣誉
但如果那女士
一世纪仅来一次,玫瑰
就变得多余——

881

I've none to tell me to but Thee
So when Thou failest, nobody.
It was a little tie—
It just held Two, nor those it held
Since Somewhere thy sweet Face has spilled
Beyond my Boundary—

If things were opposite—and Me
And Me it were—that ebbed from Thee
On some unanswering Shore—
Would'st Thou seek so—just say
That I the Answer may pursue
Unto the lips it eddied through—
So—overtaking Thee—

881

我找不到谁能告诉我除了你
所以当你说不出,就没人可以。
这是一丝联系——
它只联结两个,而非那些
自从某处你甜美的脸满溢
越出我的边际——

假如万物相互对立——而我
而我假如是——自你那里退落
在某个无人应答的海滨——
你是否希望如此——请说

我会将答案追击
追至那唇它旋转通过——
这样——就能追上你——

882

A Shade upon the mind there passes
As when on Noon
A Cloud the mighty Sun encloses
Remembering

That some there be too numb to notice
Oh God
Why give if Thou must take away
The Loved?

882

一片阴影从心头经过
像在午间
一朵乌云将骄阳紧裹
令人想起

有些无声的东西不曾引人注意
啊上帝
如果你一定要掳去那亲爱的人
为何还要给予?

883

The Poets light but Lamps—
Themselves—go out—
The Wicks they stimulate—
If vital Light

Inhere as do the Suns—

Each Age a Lens
Disseminating their
Circumference—

883

诗人们只点亮灯盏——
他们自己——走出去——
他们激励的灯芯——
如果光彩熠熠

的确天然似太阳——
每个时代就是一块镜片
把他们的光芒
撒向周边——

884

An Everywhere of Silver
With Ropes of Sand
To keep it from effacing
The Track called Land.

884

某处遍地银光熠熠
有无数绳索细如沙粒
以防它抹去
那被称为"陆地"的轨迹。

885

Our little Kinsmen—after Rain
In plenty may be seen,
A Pink and Pulpy multitude
The tepid Ground upon.

A needless life, it seemed to me
Until a little Bird
As to a Hospitality
Advanced and breakfasted.

As I of He, so God of Me
I pondered, may have judged,
And left the little Angle Worm
With Modesties enlarged.

885①
我们细小的亲戚——在雨后
大量涌现,
那桃红和多汁的族群
在微温的地面。

在我看来,是一种不必要的生命
直至一只小鸟
像是对一种殷勤的回应
向前去享用早餐。

如同我对他,上帝也这样对我
我思量,作了裁定②,
让那小小的蚯蚓
在膨胀的谦卑里忘形③。

---

① 艾米莉·狄金森1858年(富兰克林版认为是1859年)8月末写给朋友鲍尔斯的一封信中曾提到蚯蚓:"Our Pastor says we are a 'Worm.' How is that reconciled? 'Vain-sinful Worm' is possibly of another species."(L193)
② 本行与上一行原文是一句话,即"I pondered, as I have judged of He, so God may have judeged of Me."。
③ 最后一节或指如同"我"对蚯蚓作了评判,认为是多余的生命一样,上帝可能也已对"我"作了裁定。上帝对蚯蚓的评判难以为凡人知晓,也不再予以任何干预,任由蚯蚓的低调谦卑增大、膨胀,因为蚯蚓也不知自身的价值,所以"忘形"。

886

These tested Our Horizon—
Then disappeared
As Birds before achieving
A Latitude.

Our Retrospection of Them
A fixed Delight,
But our Anticipation
A Dice—a Doubt—

886①

这一些检验我们的地平线②——
然后消失不见
像鸟儿们抵达
某个纬度之前。

我们对他们的怀想
总带来欢愉,
但我们对未来的展望
是一粒骰子———一丝疑虑——

887

We outgrow love, like other things
And put it in the Drawer—
Till it an Antique fashion shows—
Like Costumes Grandsires wore.

---

① 题解:这一些死者检验我们的地平线,然后就消失不见了,正如鸟儿在到达某个目标纬度前也会消失不见一样。追念死者,总带来欢愉,展望未来,则会有疑虑,不知地平线外的情形会怎样。

② 地平线(Horizon):艾米莉·狄金森在1861年写给"主人"(Master)的一封信中用 Horizon 喻指天地间的边界线:"– and you have felt the Horizon – hav'nt you – and did the sea – never come so close as to make you dance?"(L233)

887①

我们不再需要爱，像别的东西
就把它放入抽屉——
直至它显得样式古旧——
像祖父穿的华衣。

888

When I have seen the Sun emerge
From His amazing House—
And leave a Day at every Door
A Deed, in every place—

Without the incident of Fame
Or accident of Noise—
The Earth has seemed to me a Drum,
Pursued of little Boys

888

当我看见太阳出现
自他绚烂的宫殿——
在每个门前放一个白天
每个地方，一个事件——

既无声名的插曲
也无噪音的事故——
地球于我仿佛一面鼓，
受男孩们追逐

889

Crisis is a Hair

---

① 艾米莉·狄金森 1855 年 1 月末写给嫂子苏珊的一封信里有类似抽屉的比喻："If it is finished, tell me, and I will raise the lid to my box of Phantoms, and lay one more love in."（L177）

Toward which the forces creep
Past which forces retrograde
If it come in sleep

To suspend the Breath
Is the most we can
Ignorant is it Life or Death
Nicely balancing.

Let an instant push
Or an Atom press
Or a Circle hesitate
In Circumference

It—may jolt the Hand
That adjusts the Hair
That secures Eternity
From presenting—Here—

889①
危机是一根丝发
力顺着它蔓延
力也通过它消退
假如它来时正值睡眠

我们所能做的
就是屏住呼吸
不论它是生是死

---

① 题解：英语"crisis"源于拉丁词，原意为 judgment、critical stage。本诗中的危机可视为生与死之间的边际状态，只有一根丝发的距离。生，则力涨；死，则力消。在垂死关头（"假如它来时正值睡眠"），不论结果是生是死，人只能平心静气等待。可以想象有一种力，像一只手，以瞬间之忽去推它，以原子之轻去按压它，或一个生命的轮回（圆圈）在它四周犹豫，但丝发会弹开那只手，不许它改变自己的状态。正因为有丝发，有生与死之间的距离，死亡（永恒）才不会在此时此地出现。

都要平心静气。

尽管让一瞬间来推
或一粒原子来按
或一个圆圈犹豫
在它周边

它——会弹开那只手
那手想将丝发调适
是丝发确保永恒
不在此时——显示——

890

From Us She wandered now a Year,
Her tarrying, unknown,
If Wilderness prevent her feet
Or that Ethereal Zone

No eye hath seen and lived
We ignorant must be—
We only know what time of Year
We took the Mystery.

890①

离开我们她漂泊至今已一年,
不知她在何处,驻停,

---

① 本诗写于 1864 年。约翰逊认为本诗可能是纪念艾米莉·狄金森的妈妈艾米莉·诺克罗斯(Emily Norcross Dickinson, 1804—1882)最小的弟弟乔·诺克罗斯(Joel Warren Norcross, 1821—1900)的夫人拉米拉(Lamira)的。这位米拉舅妈(Aunt Mira)比艾米莉·狄金森大 7 岁,1862 年 5 月 4 日死于肺结核病。艾米莉·狄金森可能将本诗寄给了她的两位表妹,也即拉米拉的侄女弗朗西丝·诺克罗斯和路易莎·诺克罗斯。路易莎在拉米拉去世后帮着照顾拉米拉留下的两个孩子威廉(William)和安娜(Anna)。

是否荒野阻碍了她的步履
抑或是那太虚之境

见过她的人都已不在
我们看来难以知悉——
只记得在一年中的何时
我们得到了这个谜。

891

To my quick ear the Leaves—conferred—
The Bushes—they were Bells—
I could not find a Privacy
From Nature's sentinels—

In Cave if I presumed to hide
The Walls—begun to tell—
Creation seemed a mighty Crack—
To make me visible—

891

树叶向我敏锐的耳朵——私语——
灌木丛——像钟声响起——
从大自然的哨兵那里
我没发现能有什么隐秘——

假设我藏入洞中
四壁——就开始宣布——
造物好似一道恢宏的裂缝——
让我在其中显露——

892

Who occupies this House?

A Stranger I must judge
Since No one know His Circumstance—
'Tis well the name and age

Are writ upon the Door
Or I should fear to pause
Where not so much as Honest Dog
Approach encourages.

It seems a curious Town—
Some Houses very old,
Some—newly raised this Afternoon,
Were I compelled to build

It should not be among
Inhabitants so still
But where the Birds assemble
And Boys were possible.

Before Myself was born
'Twas settled, so they say,
A Territory for the Ghosts—
And Squirrels, formerly.

Until a Pioneer, as
Settlers often do
Liking the quiet of the Place
Attracted more unto—

And from a Settlement
A Capitol has grown
Distinguished for the gravity
Of every Citizen.

The Owner of this House
A Stranger He must be—
Eternity's Acquaintances
Are mostly so—to me.

892
是谁住在这栋房?
一个陌生客我敢断定
因为没人了解他的情况——
还好姓名和年龄

都写在门上
否则我会害怕驻足
这里诚实的狗
都不太鼓励你靠近。

这看来是个怪异的城镇——
有些房子很古老,
有些——今天下午才矗起,
假如要我来建造

它不会位于
如此静默的居民里
而是鸟儿的聚集地
可能还有男孩们嬉戏。

在我出生前
已有人定居,他们这样断言,
这是鬼魂的领地——
还有松鼠,从前。

直至一位先辈,如
一般移民的常俗

喜爱此地的静穆
吸引更多人进驻——

于是从一个聚居处
发展成一个大屋
其特别之处
是每个居民都肃穆。

这栋房的房主
是陌生客无疑——
永恒的相熟
对我而言——大都如此。

893

Drab Habitation of Whom?
Tabernacle or Tomb—
Or Dome of Worm—
Or Porch of Gnome—
Or some Elf's Catacomb?

893①

这是谁淡褐色的住处?
临时的营房或坟墓——
或蠕虫的圆顶屋——
或地神的廊户——
或某位小精灵的地窟?

894

Of Consciousness, her awful Mate

---

① 本诗写于1864年。据艾米莉·狄金森的哥哥奥斯汀的女儿玛蒂的说法,艾米莉·狄金森把这首诗寄送给了奥斯汀的大儿子内德(Ned,即Edward Dickinson, 1861—1898),还随附了一个蚕茧。艾米莉·狄金森很喜欢这个侄子。

The Soul cannot be rid—
As easy the secreting her
Behind the Eyes of God.

The deepest hid is sighted first
And scant to Him the Crowd—
What triple Lenses burn upon
The Escapade from God—

894

对于知觉,她可怕的伴侣
灵魂无法脱离——
像将她藏匿于
上帝眼睛背后那么容易。

隐藏越深被发现得越快
众生几乎不入他眼里——
三倍透镜聚焦的
是逃离上帝的恶作剧——

895

A Cloud withdrew from the Sky
Superior Glory be
But that Cloud and it's Auxiliaries
Are forever lost to me

Had I but further scanned
Had I secured the Glow
In an Hermetic Memory
It had availed me now.

Never to pass the Angel
With a glance and a Bow

Till I am firm in Heaven
Is my intention now.

895
一朵云彩从天空退去
光彩熠熠
但云彩及其相关的一切
永远与我失之交臂

假如我再细看一眼
假如我将那光亮留住
在密封的记忆里
如今会对我大有益处。

决不要路过天使身旁
又鞠躬又瞥目
除非我真的上了天堂
这正是我此刻的意图。

896
Of Silken Speech and Specious Shoe
A Traitor is the Bee
His service to the newest Grace
Present continually

His Suit a chance
His Troth a Term
Protracted as the Breeze
Continual Ban propoundeth He
Continual Divorce.

896
说柔滑的语言穿俗丽的鞋子

蜜蜂是个背信弃义之徒
将他的殷勤向最新的恩惠
频频献出

他的追求都是随机
他的婚约是个期限
持续短暂如微风
他频繁公告结婚
又频繁离婚。

897

How fortunate the Grave—
All Prizes to obtain—
Successful certain, if at last,
First Suitor not in vain.

897

坟墓多么幸运——
囊括了所有荣耀——
无疑是功成名就，如果最后，
第一位追求者没有徒劳。

898

How happy I was if I could forget
To remember how sad I am
Would be an easy adversity
But the recollecting of Bloom

Keeps making November difficult
Till I who was almost bold
Lose my way like a little Child
And perish of the cold.

898
我若能忘记那该多高兴
想起我多么压抑
是一件容易的苦事
但对花开的回忆

让十一月变得难熬
直至我这个也算是胆大之士
像孩童一样迷路
并在寒冷中消逝。

899
Herein a Blossom lies—
A Sepulchre, between—
Cross it, and overcome the Bee—
Remain—'tis but a Rind.

899①
这里有一枝花——
一座坟墓,间隔——
越过它,就超越了蜜蜂——
留下——就是一副枯壳。

900
What did They do since I saw Them?
Were They industrious?
So many questions to put Them
Have I the eagerness

That could I snatch Their Faces
That could Their lips reply

---

① 题解:一枝花,越过坟墓,就可以上天堂,得永生;留在尘世,就在坟墓里干枯,只剩一副枯壳。

Not till the last was answered
Should They start for the Sky.

Not if Their Party were waiting,
Not if to talk with Me
Were to Them now, Homesickness
After Eternity.

Not if the Just suspect me
And offer a Reward
Would I restore my Booty
To that Bold Person, God—

900
自我见过他们以来他们都干啥?
他们很忙碌吗?
有这么多问题想问他们
假如我有那热情的话

比如我能否捏住他们的脸颊
他们可否用双唇回话
可否等到把最后一个问题回答
他们才向天空进发。

如果有友伴等候就别走,
如果要和我谈话就别走
假如他们现在,有乡愁
在新生之后。

先别走,假如正义对我怀疑
还给我一个奖励
我是否该把我的战利品
还给那位胆大之人,上帝——

附录 1955年集注版与1960年阅读版词汇变化一览表

序号	1955年集注版	1960年阅读版	诗序号
1	Just as the case may be—	As Deity decree—	608
2	it's	its	611、618、629、650、652、660、670、683、723、744、750、754、777、784、787、797、808、822、829、858、876、895
3	Look down upon Captivity—	Abolish his Captivity—	613
4	c'd	could	634
5	Head	Ear	634
6	Tis	'Tis	639
7	thro	thro'	648
8	'Twas	'Tis	649
9	Wo	Woe	660、708
10	vailed	veiled	663
11	'Tis'nt	'Tisn't	669
12	Lybian	Libyan	681
13	Does'nt	Doesn't	688
14	I could not see it now—	I could see it now—	692
15	Have'nt	Haven't	700
16	wont	won't	704
17	shant	shan't	704
18	thosoever	tho'soever	705
19	does'nt	doesn't	708
20	Would'nt	Wouldn't	728

续上表

序号	1955年集注版	1960年阅读版	诗序号
21	Twould	'Twould	736
22	fractured	flung it	747
23	reviled	denounced	747
24	twere	'twere	751、814
25	Her's	Hers	786
26	strategem	stratagem	786
27	Sovreign	Sovereign	791、801
28	could'nt	couldn't	793
29	Nescessity	Necessity	807
30	What Day be dark to me What Distance far	What Day be dark to me— What Distance—far—	808
31	That touch—how seldomly	That touch—how seldomly—	808
32	tho	tho'	819
33	Exhilirates	Exhilarates	838